Nemo's Fury pr

GAME OF RUNES

Book 1: The Swamp of Nok

Chris Hunneysett

Copyright © 2024 Chris Hunneysett

Illustrations & design by Chris Hunneysett

All rights reserved. This book or any portion thereof may not be reproduced, stored in a retrieval system, or transmitted in any form, or by any means (electronic, mechanical, photocopying, recording or otherwise) without the written permission of the authors.

This book is sold subject to the condition it shall not, by way of trade or otherwise, be lent, hired out, or otherwise circulated without the author's prior consent in any form of binding or cover other than that in which it is published and without a similar condition being imposed a subsequent purchaser.

The story, all names, characters, and incidents portrayed in this book are fictitious. No identification with actual persons (living or deceased), places, buildings, and products is intended or should be inferred.

Also by the same author:
Nemo's Fury (with Niall McLoughlin)
(Available from Amazon)

This is your story..

Welcome to Duros, ancient and mysterious land of magic, monsters and mayhem. And much worse.

You're an adventurer in the Fenlands of Duros, a wild frontier where only the desperate, foolhardy and dangerous dare to wander. Your name is Andi and your motto is, 'I'm Andi with or without a sword'.

It's more of a large dagger, really. Times are hard. And not one person has ever been amused by your motto, no matter how many times you've rolled it out. And it's wearing as thin as your old leather boots. Your travelling cloak has also seen better days, your tunic could do with some attention and the less said about your pants, the better.

Pigginmud is not somewhere you ever intended to end up. The village's greatest, probably only claim to fame, is it saw the demise of the feared outlaw, 'Good luck' Johnstone. He was murdered in his chair by an opportunistic barber, hired to shave Johnstone in an attempt to disguise himself from the Red Army posse.

The barber finessed his heroic deed into a successful foray into politics, and in a tightly fought contest won the position of mayor by a whisker. As the barber frequently joked afterwards, 'it was a very close shave.'

His political career came to an abrupt end when he choked on a gristle pie from the street stall next to his barber shop.

Pigginmud sits on the edge of the Swamp of Nok, and, as any wary traveller will tell you, the swamp is not for the foolhardy. It's a poisonous, malodorous place, home to creatures foul and hungry. It's true, there are indeed some folk eking out a living in the swamp, people of good heart who will offer you nothing but glad tidings. But the majority of people there will rip your arm off as soon as say hello to you.

However, as crossing the swamp is the quickest way to cross the Fenlands, many people risk its dangers to save themselves a few days of travelling by going around the swamp.

You've been hired by the terrified and clearly very desperate people of the village of Pigginmud to venture deep into the Nok Swamp to locate the fabled Goblet of Zakzak.

Legend claims that the goblet lies at the heart of the swamp, inside the Cave of Nak where one must overcome challenges of skill, strength and wit. And if you survive those, the goblet is also protected by a final magical trap of deadly artifice. No one is quite sure what these challenges consist of, as no one has ever returned to explain.

Worse, the swamp lies within a magical cataclysm which makes for capricious navigation. West does always mean west, and north rarely means north. And who really knows what south means at the best of times?

The goblet is supposedly possessed of a magical power capable of defeating any enemy. The loremasters are none too clear on how this power manifests itself, but they all agree that alcohol plays a part. An unkind observer might suggest alcohol would seem to play a great part in the loremasters' auguries.

The tyrannical Bone Baron and the Skeleton Horde are a vicious band of mercenaries and renegades who have razed three nearby villages in the past fortnight and have declared that Pigginmud will be next. They've promised they'll arrive at noon sharp tomorrow.

There are many more villages on the Bone Baron to-do list and she is even more famed for her punctuality than for her disregard for the welfare of others.

Given that the village is too small for a militia and the ruler of the Fenlands and his army are very far away, it's up to the various farriers, smiths and stallholders to defend the village. And in their wisdom, they've turned to the first adventurer who crossed the threshold of the local tavern. You are their first, last and sadly best hope of surviving the Bone Baron's attack.

The Swill Bucket is the only tavern in the village and is a small spit and sawdust place, kept by a surly landlady called Sally 'Short' Measure. Her favourite word seems to be 'off.' She liberally prefaces it with a remarkable variety of inventive and imaginative if rather unlikely and physically difficult adjectives and verbs.

'Short' Measure is ill-mannered, belligerent and not overly-familiar with the concept of personal hygiene. She's also brilliant at arithmetic, can serve a pint of ale faster than anyone else in the district and is able to spot a clipped groat at five yards. Her meaty and tattooed forearms bear testament to her adolescent years working as a docker and is more than useful with the pair of battle-axes hanging behind the bar.

The windows of the Bucket are small, ill-fitted and dirty, and many of the glass panes have been replaced by rough pieces of wood. You assume they were damaged in one of the many barfights the establishment hosts in lieu of any other entertainment. At least, that's what you surmise from the generous quantities of dried blood on the uneven flagstones.

What little light there is in the tavern is provided by a lantern above the bar, the occasional candle stump on a table, and the last embers of a never-roaring fire.

It's in The Swill Bucket you've hired a fellow desperado. Ashto Ashes is a dwarf scholar who claims to know a great deal of lore about the swamp and the goblet. In the short time he's been in the tavern he's certainly acquiring a great deal of local knowledge about the local goblets.

Ashto is tall, for a dwarf, and stout, for a dwarf, and relatively sober, for a dwarf. He's dressed in a dark green traveller's cloak and hood which is buttoned underneath his second chin. A knotted red beard flows beyond his broad black belt and to the tops of his knee-length hiking boots.

He claims to be a professor or a doctor or somesuch, from a university you didn't quite catch the name of. Nevertheless, Ashto claims to know a great deal of lore about the swamp which will be useful.

You'll be paid on return to Pigginmud only if you have the Goblet. You set off at noon. Time is running out.

How to play

You will need a six-sided dice and a pen or pencil. If you don't want to mark this book, any available piece of paper will do, or go to **gameofrunes.com** and download a copy of the adventure sheet for free.

You have five attributes; Charisma, Dexterity, Strength, Wisdom and Time. You need to keep a running total of their values on your adventure sheet (see following pages), along with any items and weapons you pick up during your adventure.

The long campaign

The Game of Runes series can played as individual adventures or as one campaign. So if you've played and survived Book 2: Marsh of Mayhem or any of the other books in the series, you may copy your Strength scores etc, your spells, weapons and all other items to use in this adventure. This will also be true of further books in the series.

Or you may begin each book completely afresh and roll new attributes. Picking your best scores and items from a previous book is not allowed. You must use **all** your old scores, spells, weapons and items, or **none** at all and begin afresh.

How to determine your initial attributes:
For your Charisma score roll **2D6** (a six-sided dice, roll twice). This will give you a number between 2 and 12. Enter this number on your adventure sheet.
Repeat for your Dexterity score.
Repeat for your Wisdom score.

To determine your Strength score roll **4D6** (a six-sided dice, roll four times), and add these rolls together to obtain a number between 4 and 24. Enter this number on your adventure sheet.

Your Time score begins at 24 and will reduce as the game instructs. If your Time reaches 0 (zero) you're out of time and your adventure is over. The game will instruct when to subtract or add to your Time score.

Combat

1. Choose a weapon from your adventure sheet. Each weapon has its own weapon score. (See the Weapon chart below for more details.) If you possess no weapon it's assumed you are using your fists so you'll always have a minimum Weapon score of 1. You begin the game armed with a shiv.

2. Add your Dexterity score to your Weapon score. This is your Initial attack score.

3. Then roll **2D6** and add this to your Initial attack score. This total is your Final attack score.

E.g. Dexterity (8) + Weapon score (2) = an Initial attack score of 10. Initial attack score (10) + 2D6 (e.g. 7) = a Final attack score of 17.

4. Now calculate your enemy's Final Attack score. Your enemy's statistics will be presented like this:

The Tinker
Initial attack score: **5**
Weapon damage: **1**
Strength: **3**

5. Roll 2D6 and add this number to their Initial attack score to create their Final attack score.
E.g. Initial attack score (5) + 2D6 (7) = Final attack score (12)

6. Calculate who has won the attack round.
Your Final attack score = 17
Tinker's Final attack score = 12
If your Final attack score is equal to or greater than your enemy's, you have won the attack round.

7. Calculate the damage you've inflicted on your enemy (or they've inflicted on you).
As you've won this attack round, subtract your chosen weapon's Weapon damage from their Strength score.
E.g. Tinker's Strength (3) - your Weapon damage (3) = Tinker's Strength (0)
(Unless instructed otherwise, your Weapon damage will be the same as your Weapon score.)

8. Go to step 1 and repeat until your enemy's strength is 0 (zero) or your Strength is 0 (zero) and the game is over.

Supplies

You begin the game with a backpack, a shiv (see Weapons chart below) and some groats. Roll **3D6** to discover how many you have.

Weapons chart

Weapons	Weapon score	Damage score
Fists	1	1
Shiv	2	2
Dagger	3	3
Club	4	4
Spiked Club	5	5
Mace	6	6
Flail	7	7
Axe	8	8
Shortsword	9	9
Sword	10	10
War Hammer	11	11
Longsword	12	12

Defence

In combat, if you suffer any damage, you must deduct your **Defence** score from the **Damage** score (so you suffer less damage), and then deduct the same amount from your **Defence** score. Once your **Defence** score reaches **0** (zero) the helmet is considered broken beyond use.

You may not use another helmet at the same time and until the helmet is broken the game assumes you are wearing and not, for example, carrying it in your bag. You may use other armour should you have it in conjunction with the helmet e.g. a breastplate or a shield, and distribute any damage among your armour.

Example 1:
You're wearing a helmet.
Your **Damage** score = 7
Your **Defence** score = 10
You deduct **7** from your **Defence** score and suffer no damage to your **Strength** score.

Example 2
You're using a shield.
Your **Damage** score = 7
Your **Defence** score = 3

You must deduct **4** from your **Strength** score and **7** from your **Defence** score. Your helmet is now useless and you must remove it from your adventure sheet.

Example 3
You have a helmet with a score of **7** and a breastplate with a score of **5**
Your **Damage** score = **7**
Your **Defence** score = **12**
You suffer no loss to your **Strength** score but must deduct a total of **7** from your total **Defence** score. You may do this in any combination you wish but if you decide your breastplate suffers all **7** points of damage, then its **Defence** score becomes **0** and you must remove it from your adventure sheet.

Spells & Magic

You can restore your attributes by using magic spells which you may be able to buy, win or steal on your adventure. You may cast spells at any time except during combat or after you've been told the game is over.

Spells chart

Hex of Knowledge	Add 2 to Wisdom
Hex of Power	Add 2 to Strength
Hex of Time	Add 1D6 to Time

Victuals

You can also restore your attributes by eating and drinking victuals which you may be able to buy, win or steal on your adventure. You may eat and/or drink at any time except during combat or after you've been told the game is over.

Food and drink are measured in rations.
1 ration will restore **2** points to your **Strength** score.
1 alcohol ration will restore **2** points to your **Strength** but will deduct one point from each of your **Dexterity** and **Wisdom** scores.
Before you set off, you may wish to buy any or none of the following items. Mark your chosen items on your adventure and adjust your number of groats accordingly.

Elf bread (**4** rations) = **11** groats
Dwarf bread (**3** rations) = **7** groats
Halfling bread (**2** rations) = **5** groats
Waterskin (**2** rations) = **5** groats
Length of rope = **5** groats
Dagger = **10** groats
Club = **15** groats

ADVENTURE SHEET

WISDOM	CHARISMA	DEXTERITY	TIME 24	STRENGTH
SPELLS		RATIONS		

WEAPON	ATTACK	DAMAGE

GROATS	ITEMS

Your adventure begins!
You enter the swamp, but which way do you go?
North? **Go to 129**
East? **Go to 40**
South? **Go to 16**

1
The orcs spot you and quickly surround you, preventing you from escaping by pointing their notched swords at you. They grunt and holler excitedly and you retch at their foul stench.
Confess? **Go to 298**
Attack? **Go to 378**

2
As you try to leave you get caught in a thick sticky strand of webbing that coats all the surrounding foliage. The more you try to wipe it off you, the more it coats your clothes and hinders your progress.
Greet? **Go to 157**
Attack? **Go to 55**

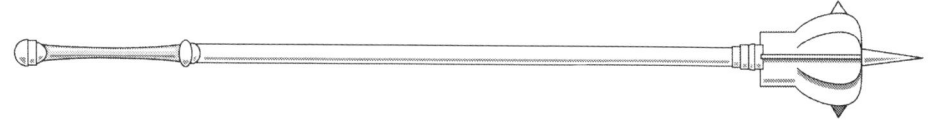

3
The silver key fits perfectly and turns smoothly in the lock. At the bottom of the iron box a small hidden door flips open and spits groats at your feet. Before you can react the door snaps shut again.

Roll **5D6** to determine how many groats you've received. **Go to 170**

4

Roll **2D6**. How does this score compare to your **Dexterity**?
Equal or higher? **Go to 245**
Lower? **Go to 100**

5

A cold wind bites at you and vultures circle overhead. Ashto mumbles, 'We should come back for that plinth. I know someone who'll pay good money for that masonry.'
Deduct **1** from your **Time** score. Out of time? **Go to 413**
Which way do you go next?
East? **Go to 68**
North? **Go to 63**
South? **Go to 53**

6

Suddenly the air begins to warm and from a shimmering green haze, a fairy appears. Piles of ragged hair fall over his translucent skin and across his sparkling knee-length tunic made of leaves. Ashto shrugs and says, 'I told you so.'

The fairy bows and says, 'Hello and listen carefully, for the faun of the swamp is an impatient and capricious character. Foolish are they who don't homage to the most powerful sorcerer of the swamp. There's no gift without pleasure, no weapon without treasure, pay homage to the great faun, or witness no dawn.'

Homage costs **1** groat. If you want to pay homage you must have at least **1** groat. If so, deduct one groat from your adventure sheet and go to that section.

Homage? **Go to 293**
Leave? **Go to 343**
Attack? **Go to 281**

7

Test your **Dexterity**. Roll **2D6**. How does this score compare to your **Dexterity**?
Equal or higher? **Go to 380**
Lower? **Go to 296**

8

Ashto rubs his beard and says, 'Be careful Andi, for the gods of the swamp are often in a most mischievous fettle. That fruit may not be what it seems. Gods are often fickle, especially the heathen ones.' Ashto looks around, gulps and says hurriedly and rather loudly, 'Of course, Xullu, the great dwarf god, the Most Major Miner of the Eternal Caverns, is always the most honourable of gods. And curse anyone who disagrees with me.'

Grasping the fruit feels like picking up an old sock. The fruit collapses into a soggy pulpy mess and maggots start crawling out of it.

Deduct **1** from your **Charisma** score.
Pluck? **Go to 227**
Leave? **Go to 408**
Attack? **Go to 242**

9

Before you can recover your breath, a swarm of Skeleton warriors appear. They swarm over you, grabbing your limbs, their bones clicking and clacking as they do so. They smell vaguely of chalk. Their faces are fixed in a permanent grin, and the clatter of their jawbones clatter makes you assume they're laughing at you. They drag you back towards Pigginmud. **Go to 230**

10

You emerge from the swamp at the foot of a rugged cliff wall where the faint heat of a weak sun falls upon your face. A cave entrance looms at the bottom of the crumbling cliff face. Vines and creepers hang over the cave mouth. A vulture wheels about overhead and somewhere not very far away, a wolf howls. A loud dripping comes from within the cave. Another wolf howls an answer to the first.

This is the Cave of Nak.
Ashto chuckles and says, 'This is more like it, a nice homely cavern!'

You step inside the cold, dank cave. The ground underneath is rocky, damp and treacherous. Water drips in the darkness and the fluttering of batwings can be heard overhead. The smell of rotting flesh makes you gag. After lighting a wooden torch with your flint, you make your way down a long and twisting tunnel, and as it coils downwards it becomes increasingly narrow so that you have to force yourself through two walls of jagged rock in order to progress. And all the while the stench of putrid| flesh becomes ever more nauseating.

Eventually, you exit the tunnel and emerge into a huge chamber. A raised drawbridge stands vertically next to a tunnel entrance on the far side of a deep chasm. It's so deep you can't see or even guess how far down it goes.

Without being able to lower the drawbridge, the only means of crossing the chasm is a long single wooden plank which crosses the gap. There's an iron hook attached to the ceiling which may help you cross but only if you have a length of rope.

Ashto laughs loudly and exclaims, 'Chasms don't scare me, we dwarves love the great deeps of the world. We were born in darkness and we'll die in darkness, there's nothing for me to fear here! You go first.'

How will you cross?

Rope? **Go to 49**

Hex of Drawing? **Go to 149**

Plank? **Go to 58**

11

Test your **Dexterity**. Roll **2D6**. How does this score compare to your **Dexterity**?

Equal or higher? **Go to 387**

Lower? **Go to 111**

12

You carry on your journey, wondering how many more orcs are wandering the land. Ashto curses and says, 'We must murder every orc we encounter! Every one of them, do you hear me?'
Deduct **1** from your **Time** score. Out of time? **Go to 413**
Which way do you go next?
North? **Go to 84**
East? **Go to 75**
West? **Go to 93**

13

You catch the flame in your fist but feel no pain as instantly the flame disappears and a **Charisma** spell drops out of the plinth into one of the trays. Mark this on your adventure sheet.
Ashto says, 'Never has anyone needed that more than you.'
Go to 259

14

Ashto yells, 'Time hates us!'
Deduct **1** from your **Time** score. Out of time? **Go to 413**
Which way do you go next?
East? **Go to 33**
West? **Go to 43**
North? **Go to 48**

15

You search the forester and find three items. You can choose only one to take with you. You may take nothing if you wish.

Ashto groans, 'I can't believe we risked our lives for this! This!'

Make your choice:

A bunch of freshly cut Sogweed

An **AXE**

A small jar of Howlmeat

Go to 121

16

Many birds take flight from the great oak trees as a peal of thunder echoes through the swamp, and a moment later a lightning bolt sears the dark sky.

The lightning draws your attention to a gnarly old fruit tree standing at the side of the path. Its bark is nearly black with age and is covered with a wide variety of moss and lichen. Mice and voles scurry across its ancient roots and squirrels and birds are making considerable noise in its heavy and leafy boughs.

Ashto strokes his beard thoughtfully and mutters, 'This is clearly a tree of very powerful magic, some of the fruit will be wholesome and full of sustenance. Others will be less so, and possibly harmful. May the swamp gods be merciful on you.'

Avoid? **Go to 44**

Investigate? **Go to 252**

Attack? **Go to 242**

17

Test your **Dexterity**. Roll **2D6**. How does this score compare to your **Dexterity**?
Equal or higher? **Go to 409**
Lower? **Go to 265**

18

The giant swamp spiders chirp as they bustle towards you on their thick hairy legs, their stench is almost overpowering in its severity. The most hairy spider chitters, 'You smell good enough to eat!'
Chat? **Go to 42**
Attack? **Go to 387**

19

You memorise the incantation written in the book and Ashto listens intently as you chant the spell uncertainly at the portal.

Ashto's eyes widen as the flames leap higher and you feel a dramatic increase in temperature on your skin. You slowly walk towards the flames, which roar thunderously, yet allow you to pass through the portal unscathed.

Ashto scurries through the portal on your heels. **Go to 138**

20

Ashto grunts, 'Fauns are weird. Did I ever tell you about the time I rescued the daughter of a faun from the Copelands from pirates? A most interesting experience, whose successful outcome, and it was a most successful outcome, relied on my prodigious knowledge of the runes of the Silver Sea. They're a little studied rune system but my book learning saved the young faun from a most unfortunate fate. Well done me, I say!'

Deduct **1** from your **Time** score. Out of time? **Go to 413**
Which way do you go next?
West? **Go to 33**
East? **Go to 48**
South? **Go to 43**

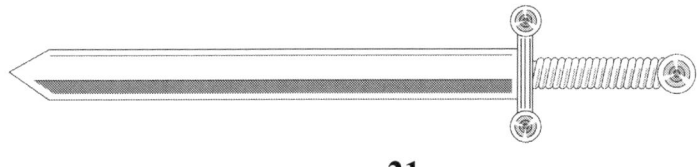

21

The swamp water is knee-deep and frequently washes over the top of your boots, and slops about your feet. Your socks are sodden and cold. You hope there are no swamp snakes or piranhas in this part of the It crosses your mind that alligators may also be lurking among the floating tree branches.

Ashto grabs your elbow and points and hisses, 'Look! These are evil creatures, filthy beasts!'

Scuttling through the swamp is a nest of goblins.

Avoid? **Go to 270**
Greet? **Go to 291**
Attack? **Go to 175**

22

A beam of sunlight bursts out from the heavy clouds and warms your body and spirits in the dank swamp. Ashto grins and slaps you on the back. He likes you!
Roll **1D6** and add the result to your **Strength**.
Roll **1D6** and add the result to your **Time**.
Go to 63

23

The swamp has become hot and sticky, increasing the smell of rotting eggs, which makes you retch. Occasionally you stumble into knee-deep water and climb out, covered in reeds, slime and frog spawn.

If you've already killed the forester, **go to 121**. If not, continue.

A forester is striding in your direction. Ashto grumbles, 'What sort of a person wants to spend their working life in a place such as this? I don't feel we can trust this person. They surely have no education.'
Avoid? **Go to 130**
Greet? **Go to 167**
Attack? **Go to 51**

24

The forester has seen you! Ashto gulps several times. **Go to 158**

25

You push pregnant women and small children out of your way in your hurry to escape the incoming Skeleton Horde.

Ashto screams, 'Get out of my way, you idiots!'

You race away into the trees beyond the village and over your shoulder you see a red mist rise above Pigginmud as the Skeleton Horde descends upon the defenceless villagers.

Ashto counts his groats and scowls, 'I can't believe this is all we were paid. It's daylight robbery is what it is. Is this all a university education worth these days? I'd be better off working down the mines.'
Which way do you go?
Left? **Go to 411**
Right? **Go to 376**
Straight ahead? **Go to 64**

26

The rain falls in huge fat drops then suddenly stops and the sun breaks through the grey clouds to warm and dry you.

If you've already killed the minstrel, **go to 154**, if not, carry on.

A minstrel whistles merrily and plays a lute as they stroll through the swamp. The female faun is wearing a frilly black silk shirt and skin-tight red leather trousers, with a scarlet wide-brimmed cavalier hat sporting a luxurious peacock feather and a long red silk scarf.

Ashto mumbles something about preferring percussion to the sound of strings.
Avoid? **Go to 236**
Greet? **Go to 278**
Attack? **Go to 271**

27

The flame disappears before you have a chance to catch it and a red jet of flame shoots out of the nearest nozzle on the side of the plinth and burns you! Ashto points and laughs at you. Roll **1D6** and deduct it from your **Strength** score. Dead? **Play again!** Alive? **Go to 259**

28

The flame disappears before you can catch it, and a red flame shoots out of the nearest nozzle on the side of the plinth and burns you. Ashto laughs. Roll **1D6** and deduct it from your **Strength** score. Dead? **Play again!** Alive? **Go to 5**

29

You've wandered into a shaded dell, the grass-covered ground is firm underfoot and there's a faint smell of peppermint in the air. A statue created out of many pieces of wood in the image of a faun stands at its centre. It dominates the surrounding trees and foliage as if it's a warning of what may befall them if they displease the gods of the swamp. Or casually insult a forester. Easily over ten feet tall, the wooden faun holds a gleaming longsword above its head. Its other hand is outstretched as if waiting to receive a gift.

Ashto grumbles, 'This faun is obviously a spirit created from very powerful magic, and we must pay homage in order to be judged worthy of receiving a gift. No doubt a spirit will be along shortly to explain this all to us.'
Avoid? **Go to 186**
Greet? **Go to 159**
Attack? **Go to 73**

30

Test your **Dexterity**. Roll **2D6**. How does this score compare to your **Dexterity**?
Equal or higher? **Go to 190**
Lower? **Go to 113**

31

You try to strike the sundial but it's protected by a powerful magic spell which reverses your power back at you. You're blasted to the ground where you roll in agony, clutching your torso. Your eyes are watering and your chest feels as if it's been smashed by a sledgehammer. Ashto can't believe his eyes at your stupidity.

Roll **1D6** and subtract that from your **Strength**.
Dead? **Play again!** Alive? You need at least **1** groat to play this game. Deduct **1** groat from your adventure sheet if you decide to play.
Play? **Go to 152**
Leave? **Go to 41**

32

The brigand has spotted you and turns and points! Roll **2D6**. How does this score compare to your **Charisma**?
Lower? **Go to 45**
Equal or higher? **Go to 135**

33

The muddy ground sinks beneath your feet and makes progress slow, and each footstep you take leaves a puddle of dirty water behind. You're leaving an easy trail for anyone who may be hunting you.

In a gap between the trees stands a nine-sided stone plinth.

Ashto grunts, 'Who's leaving a decent bit of stonework like that lying about? Someone will have that away if they're not careful.'
Avoid? **Go to 338**
Investigate? **Go to 89**
Attack? **Go to 221**

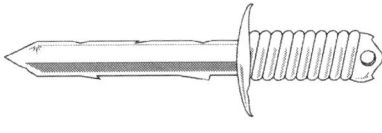

34

The brigands have spotted you! Ashto whimpers and moves to stand behind you, shaking slightly, and clutching your cloak.
Greet? **Go to 313**
Attack? **Go to 202**

35

Ashto pulls at his beard and cries, 'Of all the stupid and useless creatures!' You search the trolls for booty and find the following. You may take one at most of the following items:

A bag containing **1D6** groats

A tin crown

A femur. Possibly from a human.

Go to 395

36

Test your **Dexterity**. Roll **2D6**. How does this score compare to your **Dexterity**?

Equal or higher? **Go to 204**

Lower? **Go to 86**

37

Ashto grins and says, 'I do like a slice of fruit!'

Are the fruit gods in a mischievous fettle? Is this a trap or a trick? You hold your breath and grasp the fruit. Nothing untoward happens. Plucking the fruit feels like nothing more dangerous than plucking a fruit. You tuck it away for later. Add your chosen fruit to your adventure sheet. This piece of fruit is worth **1** ration. **Go to 408**

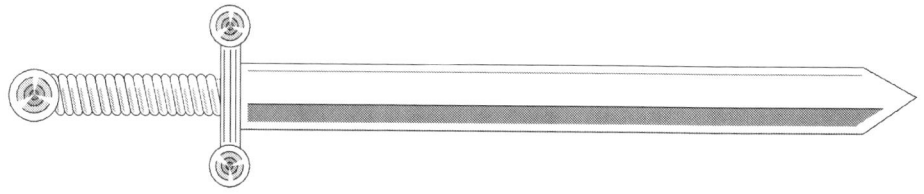

38

The forester has seen you! Ashto frowns. **Go to 16**

39

Ashto scratches his beard and mumbles, 'Nothing good ever came from a giant swamp spider.'

You ignore the foul stench rising from the hot and steamy body of the bleeding corpse of the spider as you search it for booty. You roll the spider over with a great heave. Strapped to its bloated stomach is one of the following items. Make your choice and remember to write it on your adventure sheet.

A length of string

A brass key

A loaf of dwarf bread (Worth **2** rations)

Go to 72

40

A gentle, almost mist-like rain falls on you, turning the firm ground, soft. A pair of brigands are lurking among the trees in a nearby clearing and are warming themselves by a miserly fire. Their cloaks are shabby and need repair, and their boots are caked in mud.

Ashto groans but does so quietly so only you can hear him.

Avoid? **Go to 174**

Greet? **Go to 313**

Attack? **Go to 202**

41

Ashto scratches at his beard and mutters, 'Time is fleet-footed! We must catch up!'

Deduct **1** from your **Time** score. Out of time? **Go to 413**

Which way do you go next?

South? **Go to 75**

North? **Go to 84**

West? **Go to 93**

42

Roll **2D6.** How does this score compare to your **Charisma?**

Lower? **Go to 180**

Equal or higher? **Go to 387**

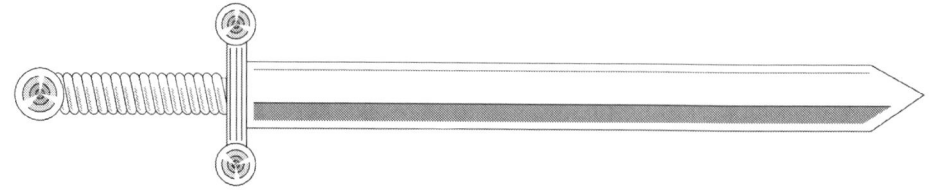

43

The ground is soggy and the trees have a strong musty smell. Many large yellow-headed mushrooms grow in their roots, and clouds of flies make a nuisance of themselves as you plod along.

If you've already killed the witch, **go to 137**. If not, continue.

Hobbling towards you is a witch. She's wearing a dark grey cotton jerkin, black breeches with a pair of brown leather boots, a dark grey bandana and a dark grey cloak.

Ashto mutters, 'Witches aren't anything but trouble. I've met a few but never one you can trust.'
Avoid? **Go to 76**
Greet? **Go to 128**
Attack? **Go to 334**

44

As you hurry past the fruit tree, Ashto sneakily tries to snatch one but they remain out of his reach. The dwarf stares longingly at the fruit over his shoulder as you hurry along. **Go to 408**

45

The brigand stands up. She's a human wearing mismatched boots and a long travelling cloak clasped at the neck with a small bronze brooch, and a deep hood hides her face. Worn and dirty leather hunting gloves protect her hands.

She moves slowly forward with one hand firmly grasping the hilt of her dagger as she approaches. She looks you slowly up and down and growls, 'You're a long way from safety. This swamp isn't safe for the unwary.'

Ashto shivers.

Chat? **Go to 209**
Leave? **Go to 144**
Attack? **Go to 135**

46

The cog turns very smoothly and you offer a silent prayer to the gods. But looking up to the ceiling instead of seeing the goblet being lowered, a vicious blade is flying towards you! Deduct **2** from your **Strength** score. Dead? **Play again!**

Alive? Continue. Ashto is bent double with his arms arched over his head and is whimpering slightly. Your life may depend on this next decision. Which cog do you turn?

Cog 1? **Go to 213**
Cog 2? **Go to 83**
Cog 4? **Go to 161**
Cog 5? **Go to 239**
Cog 6? **Go to 311**
Cog 7? **Go to 246**
Cog 8? **Go to 323**
Cog 9? **Go to 285**

47

You drop a groat into the stone slot and a bright green flame bursts from the nozzle on top of the plinth and you make swipe at it.

Test your **Dexterity**. Roll **2D6**. How does this score compare to your **Dexterity**?
Lower? **Go to 257**
Equal or higher? **Go to 28**

48

You draw your cloak tight around you as the wind whips about, engulfing you with the smell of dead sheep, dried sweat and fresh dung. A gang of bickering swamp trolls blocks the path ahead. Each troll is enormous, the girth and height of a young oak tree, and their craggy, granite features and deep eye sockets tell you they have seen many winters.

Ashto mutters, 'I never heard one good thing about trolls. Especially swamp trolls.'

Avoid? **Go to 217**
Greet? **Go to 102**
Attack? **Go to 94**

49

If you do NOT possess a length of rope, **go to 10** Otherwise, continue. You make a noose in the rope and throw it upwards, aiming the noose for the iron hook.

You hope that holding onto the suspended rope will help you balance on the wooden plank and thus more safely cross the seemingly bottomless chasm.

Test your **Dexterity**. Roll **2D6**. How does this score compare to your **Dexterity**?

Equal or higher? **Go to 240**
Lower? **Go to 216**

50

The orcs are highly trained fighting machines. And cruel with it. They don't know the meaning of the word 'mercy'. Or 'abrogate'.

Ashto pretends to kick you in the stomach, crying, 'Quick, hit them while they're down!'

Fight each orc in turn. When you've defeated the first orc you may pick up their short sword and use it in combat. Remember to add it to your adventure sheet.

Orc warrior 1
Initial attack score: **14**
Weapon damage: **9**
Strength: **9**

Orc warrior 2
Initial attack score: **15**
Weapon damage: **9**
Strength: **10**

Orc warrior 3
Initial attack score: **16**
Weapon damage: **9**
Strength: **11**

Dead? **Play again!** Win? **Go to 272**

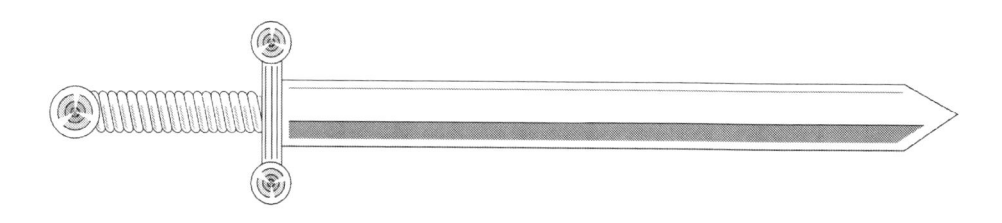

51

Ashto faints as the forester pumps their prodigious muscles and swings their axe. Fight!
Forester
Initial attack score: **14**
Weapon damage: **8**
Strength: **16**
Lose? **Play again!** Win? **Go to 15**

52

Ashto pulls at his beard and cries, 'Nothing good was ever found in an orc's pocket.'

Your hand slides gingerly into the orc's clothes. Ignoring the blood and the sweat and fleas, your fingers reach about. You hope to find something that will make this thoroughly unpleasant exercise worthwhile. Among the orc's possessions, you find some items of value and you may take one of the following items:
A length of rope
A **SHORTSWORD**
A wineskin with white wine (worth **5** alcohol rations)
Go to 12

53

A sudden downpour causes you and Ashto to huddle under the branches of an ancient willow tree. The willow is struck by a bolt of lightning strikes, breaking a large branch and showering you with electric sparks. The branch catches fire and drops towards you.

Dodging the bough you go further off the path into the thicker, and stumbling blindly through reeds and willow branches swamp, you almost fall into a silent, mist-covered grove. In the grove's centre stands an ancient lichen-covered stone sundial balanced on a crumbling stone pedestal.

Ashto grabs your arm, 'This is a most magical place. Let's not tarry.'

Avoid? **Go to 140**
Investigate? **Go to 66**
Attack? **Go to 31**

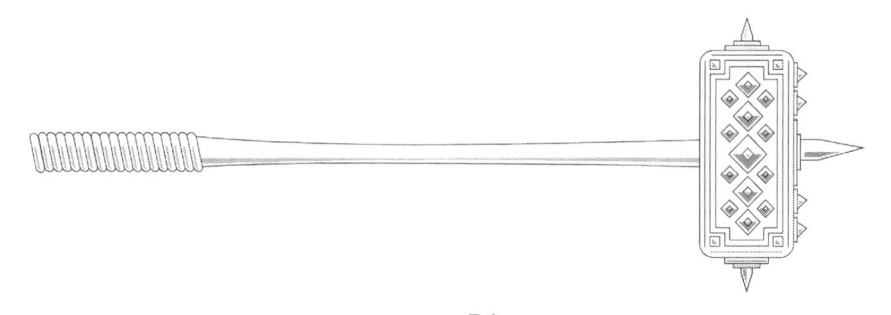

54

Ashto grunts, 'I hate foresters.'

Deduct **1** from your **Time** score. Out of time? **Go to 413**
Which way do you go next?
West? **Go to 147**
South? **Go to 382**
North? **Go to 375**

SUNDIAL

55

The spider scuttles forward to attack you with its poisonous fangs! Ashto throws his arms out and pretends to be a rather short scarecrow.

Fight! If you possess a jar of Sogweed you may smash it on the ground and the fumes which are poisonous to spiders will cause the over-sized arachnid to flee. **Go to 72** and remember to deduct the Sogweed from your adventure sheet.

If you have no Sogweed, you must fight.

Giant swamp spider
Initial attack score: **7**
Weapon damage: **5**
Strength: **22**
Dead? **Play again!** Win? **Go to 39**

56

As you walk away the wizard calls out, 'It's very rude to turn your back on a wizard! Not to mention very bad luck.' And you feel a tingling down your spine and into your legs as the wizard casts a spell on you. Deduct **1** from your **Charisma** score. Deduct **2** from your **Dexterity** score. Deduct **2** from your **Time** score.
Out of time? **Go to 413**
Deduct **4** from your **Strength** score. Dead? **Play again!**
Alive? **Go to 260**

SWAMP TROLL

57

You search the brigand but you don't expect to find anything of value, or indeed, find anything that might be said to belong to the brigand.

You find three items but can choose only one to take with you.

Ashto sighs, 'I'm always ready for an ale and a song.'

Make your choice:

An iron helmet (**Defence score = 1D6**)

3 bottles of ale (Worth **1** alcohol ration each)

A **FLAIL**

When you're ready decide what to do next. **Go to 82**

58

You tentatively step out onto the bridge and only then do you see the wooden planks are rotten with damp and insect infestation.

Test your **Dexterity**. Roll **2D6**. How does this score compare to your **Dexterity**?

Equal or higher? **Go to 240**

Lower? **Go to 109**

59

You never imagined spiders grew so big or so ferocious. Ashto curses and says, 'Spiders are a curse of the elvish gods sent to punish dwarves for our love of silver. And our love of diamonds. And rubies. And emeralds. And general digging. Curse those elvish heathen gods.'

Deduct **1** from your **Time** score. Out of time? **Go to 413**
Which way do you go next?
North? **Go to 122**
East? **Go to 126**
West? **Go to 133**

60

The witch taps you heavily on the shoulder and cries, 'Speak up! Do you want to buy a hex?'
You'll need a minimum of **15** groats to buy a hex.
Buy? **Go to 119**
Leave? **Go to 137**
Attack? **Go to 334**

61

Searching the goblins is hugely unpleasant due to their ferociously poor personal hygiene. And you're careful not to get any of their blood on your clothes.

You find three items. You can choose only one to take with you.

Ashto groans, 'All that effort, for this!'
Make your choice:
A **SWORD**
2 bottles of ale (Worth **3** alcohol rations each)
1D6 groats
Go to 14

62

The goblins change direction to scuttle towards you. Small, wiry, snaggletoothed and filthy, they're covered in rough tattoos indicating their allegiance to the Bone Baron.

The vilest one sniffs you and sniggers, 'Have you been allowed out of your kennel for a walk in the meadow?'

Ashto maintains a dignified silence and the goblins hoot and shriek, scuttling about and prodding you with the points of their weapons.

Chat? **Go to 192**
Leave? **Go to 407**
Attack? **Go to 349**

63

Between the thick trunks of ancient oaks, you glimpse a party of orcs. They're heavily armed and sporting the warpaint livery of the Bone Baron. Ashto mutters, 'Curse these orcs! We should destroy them. Every one of them. We must show no mercy.'

Avoid? **Go to 108**
Greet? **Go to 248**
Attack? **Go to 378**

64

Three armoured trolls crash through the trees, swinging their war hammers and bellowing like demented bison. You prepare to defend yourself. Ashto runs off into the trees, screaming.

Fight each troll in turn. You may use Howlmeat if you have it. One jar of howlmeat is sufficient to poison one troll and kill it. Remember to deduct each jar of howlmeat from your adventure sheet that you use.

As soon as you kill the first troll you may pick up their war hammer and use it as a weapon. Remember to add it to your adventure sheet. Fight!

Swamp troll 1
Initial attack score: **12**
Weapon damage: **11**
Strength: **21**

Swamp troll 2
Initial attack score: **13**
Weapon damage: **11**
Strength: **20**

Swamp troll 3
Initial attack score: **14**
Weapon damage: **11**
Strength: **22**

Dead? **Play again!** Win? **Go to 9**

65

Test your **Dexterity**. Roll **2D6**. How does this score compare to your **Dexterity**?

Equal or higher? **Go to 367**
Lower? **Go to 306**

66

The stone sundial has a thin brass shadow-casting arm at its centre and at each of the nine points of the circle is groat-sized slot.

Ashto scrutinises the sundial and says, 'This is obviously a shrine to the gods of Time. We must pay homage to the gods by placing a groat in a slot of our choosing, and if the gods are feeling beneficent they may bless us with more time to accomplish our mission.

'I've studied sundials such as this and we stand to gain at least a dozen hours if we choose the correct section! Not even a person of your limited intelligence can mess this up!'

You need at least **1** groat to play this game. Deduct **1** groat from your adventure sheet if you decide to play.

Play? **Go to 152**
Leave? **Go to 41**
Attack? **Go to 31**

67

Ashto scratches at his beard and moans, 'Time is leaping! We must proceed with utmost urgency!'

Deduct **1** from your **Time** score. Out of time? **Go to 413**
Which way do you go next?
South? **Go to 99**
East? **Go to 107**
North? **Go to 275**

68

Dark clouds gather overhead and rain begins to fall, at first light, but becoming heavier. You pull your hood over your head and gather your cloak around you, but you're quickly wet through. If you've already killed the wizard, **go to 260**. If not, continue.

A large puff of red smoke appears before you! When it clears a wizard stands there, peering over half-moon spectacles as he tries not to fart. He's a minotaur and is wearing a dark grey shirt with light grey trousers, a pair of tall black leather boots, a dark grey wide-brimmed hat with a tall point and a long flowing grey winter cloak.

Ashto mumbles, 'Magic, pah! That's not real scholarship. Just conjuring tricks and sleight of hand!'

Avoid? **Go to 4**
Greet? **Go to 211**
Attack? **Go to 143**

69

You pour a measure of red wine into the goblet and then putting the goblet to your lips, guzzle the ale down. Immediately you feel a surge of magical power flow through your body.

During this combat only, instead of rolling **2D6** to calculate your **Attack Score**, automatically add **12** points to your **Attack Score.**

The sheriff hands you a longsword and taking the formidable weapon, you run forwards to confront the Bone Baron!

From behind Ashto yells, 'Best of luck, if you survive I'll meet you in Tickscab village, in a tavern called The Fleeced Patron!' And the dwarf runs away. **Go to 230**

70

The emerald fairy smiles and says, 'You have been judged faithful to the eternal faun. Now prepare yourself for your reward.'

Ashto's eyes light up as three strong wooden green chests appear on the grass before you.

You may take one or none of the following. Make sure you write your choice on your adventure sheet.

A vial of Fleshrot potion

An **AXE**

A purse containing **10** groats

Go to 20

71

A mysterious force prevents you from leaving the plinth.
Go to 89

72

You never imagined spiders grew so big or so ferocious. Ashto curses and says, 'Spiders are a curse of the gods sent to punish dwarves for our love of gold!'

Deduct **1** from your **Time** score. Out of time? **Go to 413**
Which way do you go next?

West? **Go to 99**
East? **Go to 107**
North? **Go to 322**

73

The wooden faun steps forward and attacks! Ashto pretends to be a shrub. Fight!
Wooden Faun
Initial attack score: **18**
Weapon damage: **12**
Strength: **6**
Lose? **Play again!** Win? **Go to 20**

74

Choose either an apple, an orange or a banana to pluck.
Test your **Dexterity**. Roll **2D6**. Is this score higher, lower or equal to your **Dexterity**?
Higher? **Go to 297**
Equal? **Go to 373**
Lower? **Go to 359**

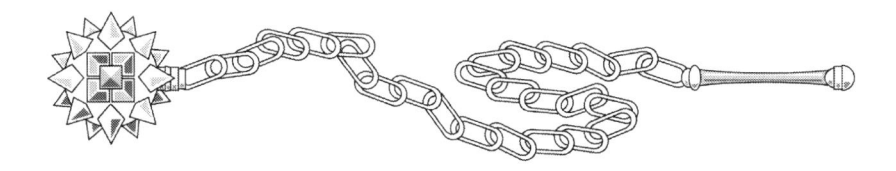

75

The swamp water is ankle deep and you slosh your way through it. An iron chest stands in the middle of a raised clearing to your left.
Avoid? **Go to 120**
Investigate? **Go to 294**
Attack? **Go to 299**

76

Test your **Dexterity**. Roll **2D6**. How does this score compare to your **Dexterity**?
Equal or higher? **Go to 354**
Lower? **Go to 88**

77

The forester pretends not to see you and carries on their journey. Ashto is sweating and fanning himself with a hand to cool down.
Go to 121

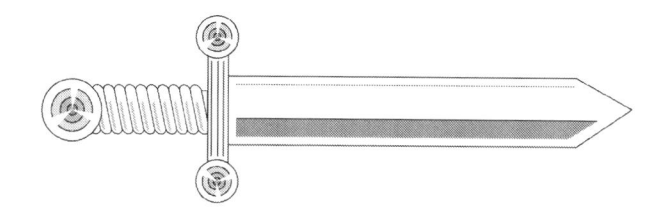

78

You search the minstrel and find three items. You can choose only one to take with you.

Ashto chuckles and says, 'We should definitely take the red wine,

it's most intellectually stimulating!'
Make your choice:
A bottle of red wine (Worth **6** alcohol rations)
A lute, worn, rather battered and now missing three strings
1D6 groats
When you're ready decide what to do next. **Go to 67**

79

Having successfully reached the far side of the chasm you lean against the rocky wall and rest for a moment.

Ashto laughs and declares, 'Chasms, I love a good chasm! And finely crafted single-span bridges made of stone. And did I ever tell you about the bridges of the Cleft Mountain realm? Mullu Longshaft, the Lord Low of the High has created in his kingdom of Deep Peak an underground paradise of finely pointed stonework decorated in intricate with many reliefs of highly artistic subject matter. It's a miracle of modern construction and visionary integrity. If you were a dwarf I'd be happy to escort you on a tour. And for a most reasonable fee.'
Deduct **1** from your **Time** score. Out of time? **Go to 413**
Alive? **Go to 156**

80

You try to strike the tree but it's protected by a powerful magic spell which reverses your power back at you. Ashto laughs at you.
Roll **1D6** and subtract that from your **Strength**.

Dead? **Play again!** Alive? What do you do?

Pluck? **Go to 145**

Leave? **Go to 324**

81

Ashto scratches at their moustache and mumbles, 'Time is fleeting! We must be swift!'

Deduct **1** from your **Time** score. Out of time? **Go to 413**

Which way do you go next?

North? **Go to 40**

East? **Go to 21**

South? **Go to 23**

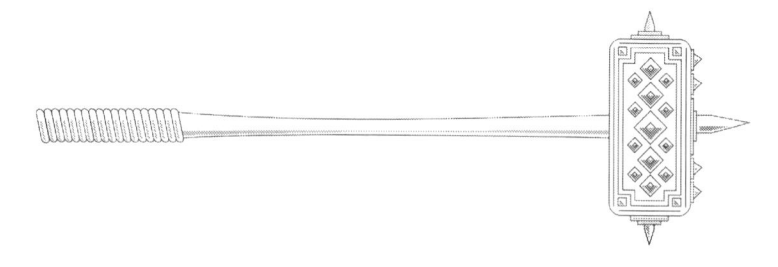

82

Ashto pulls at his beard and mutters, 'Time is leaving us behind! We must get busy!'

Deduct **1** from your **Time** score. Out of time? **Go to 413**

Which way do you go next?

West? **Go to 33**

East? **Go to 43**

South? **Go to 48**

83

The cog turns easily and so silently you can hear the faintest 'pfft' of a pneumatic device firing a devilishly sharp blade at you. Deduct **1** from your **Strength** score. Dead? **Play again!**

Alive? Continue.

At the edge of the room, Ashto has his eyes covered. Your life may depend on this next decision. Which cog do you turn?

Cog 1? **Go to 213**
Cog 3? **Go to 46**
Cog 4? **Go to 161**
Cog 5? **Go to 239**
Cog 6? **Go to 311**
Cog 7? **Go to 246**
Cog 8? **Go to 323**
Cog 9? **Go to 285**

84

Through the tree trunks, creepers and crisscrossing of webs you spy the nest of a giant swamp spider. It's huge, hairy and mottled, with poison dripping from their enormous fangs.

Ashto whispers, 'I hate spiders! Even the small ones. And especially beasts the size of cattle.'

Avoid? **Go to 268**
Greet? **Go to 157**
Attack? **Go to 55**

85

You pour an ale into the goblet and then putting the goblet to your lips, guzzle the ale down. Immediately you feel a surge of magical power flow through your body. Your **Dexterity** is now **12**.

The sheriff hands you a longsword and taking the formidable weapon, you stride forward to confront the Bone Baron!

From behind you, Ashto calls, 'Good luck, and I hope to meet you in the afterlife!' And the dwarf runs away. **Go to 230**

86

The tinker doesn't see you and you carry on your journey. Ashto breathes a rather loud and obvious sigh of relief. **Go to 352**

87

Ashto grunts, 'Fauns are weird. I've spent a great deal of time among them in the Copelands, I know what I'm talking about.'
Deduct **1** from your **Time** score. Out of time? **Go to 413**
Which way do you go next?
South? **Go to 122**
North? **Go to 133**
West? **Go to 146**

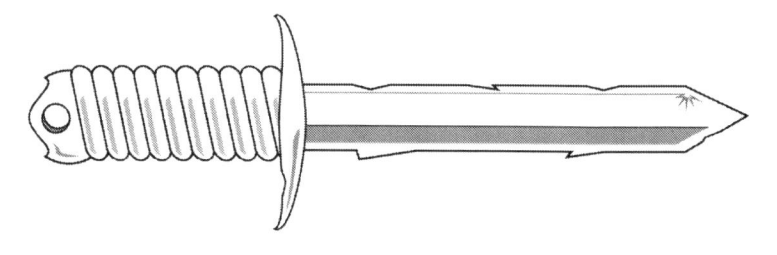

88

Ashto is manically tiptoeing away from the witch and you struggle to keep pace and keep quiet as you make your way forward.
Go to 137

89

Greatly overgrown and much weather-worn, the nine-sided stone plinth is waist-high to an average-sized adult halfling, and about halfway down each side there's a small iron nozzle pointing outwards.

Beneath each of these is a small stone tray designed to catch any objects deposited from a chute hidden within the plinth. On the top of the plinth is an inscription, beside which is a groat-sized slot and beside that is a second smaller iron nozzle, blackened around the edges.

The inscription is written in the common runes and says, 'Pay tribute to the gods and challenge the odds. Catch the flame or suffer the pain.'

Ashto declares, 'Obviously what you must do is put a groat into the slot and that activates a holy flame which the supplicant must grasp in their hand. The virtuous will be rewarded, and the sinners and undeserving will be punished. It's obviously a trap for the unworthy.'

If you want to pay tribute you must have at least one groat. If so, deduct one groat from your adventure sheet and go to that section.

Tribute? **Go to 47**
Leave? **Go to 5**
Attack? **Go to 221**

90

The bloated and stinking spider waves a leg at you and chitters, 'There's a wizard at large in the west of the swamp, and a very powerful swamp it is too. Many of our brothers and sisters have been killed by this cruel and cowardly creature. Never trust a wizard!'

Attack? **Go to 55**
Leave? **Go to 268**

91

The wizard chuckles and offers you the following. (The game will tell you when you may use these very specific spells.)

Hex of Drawing = **10** groats
Hex of Clouds = **15** groats
Hex of Framing = **20** groats

Ashto strokes his beard and muses, 'Hmm, these must be powerful spells or possibly a filthy conjurer's trick, I don't recognise any of these spells.'

You may buy one of the spells. Remember to add the time to your adventure sheet and deduct the groats.

If you can't afford to buy a hex or you choose not to: **Go to 56**
If you do buy, decide what to do next:

Attack? **Go to 143**
Leave? **Go to 260**

92

The brigand doesn't see you and you carry on your journey.

GIANT SWAMP SPIDER

Ashto grins broadly. **Go to 144**

93

The rain stops and the day warms a little, but this causes a fog to rise from the swamp, and you're forced to slog through the knee-high water with very little visibility. You frequently catch your head on low-hanging branches and are bitten by tiny insects, rising from the swamp's surface in the warm air.

If you've killed the minstrel already, **go to 67**, if not, carry on.

A minstrel is whistling pleasantly and strumming a lute as they stroll through the swamp. A faun by species, she's wearing a frilly black silk shirt and skin-tight red leather trousers, with a scarlet wide-brimmed cavalier hat sporting a luxurious peacock feather and a long red silk scarf.

Ashto mumbles something about not liking the sound of lutes.
Avoid? **Go to 134**
Greet? **Go to 370**
Attack? **Go to 148**

94

The nearest troll raises their war hammer to attack! Ashto lies down and pretends to be dead. Fight each troll in turn. You may use Howlmeat if you have it. One jar of howlmeat is sufficient to poison one troll and kill it. Remember to deduct each jar of howlmeat from your adventure sheet as you use it.

As soon as you kill the first troll you may pick up their war hammer and use it as a weapon if you wish. Remember to add it to your adventure sheet. Fight!

Swamp troll 1

Initial attack score: **12**

Weapon damage: **11**

Strength: **21**

Swamp troll 2

Initial attack score: **13**

Weapon damage: **11**

Strength: **20**

Swamp troll 3

Initial attack score: **14**

Weapon damage: **11**

Strength: **22**

Dead? **Play again!** Win? **Go to 35**

95

The shabbiest goblin spits and snickers, 'Go back to Pigginmud or Little Sibling or Lower Sog or wherever you're from before the Skeleton Horde find you.'

Leave? **Go to 14**

Attack? **Go to 175**

96

You step forward to the emerald fairy and hand over a groat, who smiles and bows and says, 'Are you a devout follower of the eternal faun? You are about to be tested. The faithless will be punished most severely but the rewards are rich for the devoted.'

Test your **Charisma**. Roll **2D6**. How does this score compare to your **Charisma**?
Lower? **Go to 187**
Equal or higher? **Go to 190**

97

The forester looks amused, holds up a vial of cloudy elixir and asks, 'Do you wish to buy a small vial of Griffdum?'

Ashto says, 'Hmm, a very useful potion rumoured to have formidable properties. Very useful against goblins, I understand.'

If you buy the elixir, deduct **15** groats from your adventure sheet and add the elixir.
Attack? **Go to 51**
Leave? **Go to 121**

98

Ashto grunts, 'I hate foresters.'
Deduct **1** from your **Time** score. Out of time? **Go to 413**
Which way do you go next?
North? **Go to 126**
East? **Go to 146**
South? **Go to 133**

99

Through the tree trunks, creepers and crisscrossing of webs you spy a nest of giant swamp spiders. They're huge, hairy and mottled, with hate emanating from their sweaty open pores.

Ashto whispers, 'Uurgh! Spiders hate dwarves! Even the big ones. And the weird dwarves that shave. I once met a dwarf who shaved. Horrible looking thing they were. Looked alarmingly like a short human.' And Ashto shudders.

Avoid? **Go to 11**
Greet? **Go to 18**
Attack? **Go to 387**

100

Ashto is grinning madly as you sneak away from the wizard. Add **1** to your **Charisma** score. **Go to 260**

101

Roll **2D6**. How does this score compare to your **Dexterity**?
Equal or higher? **Go to 290**
Lower? **Go to 314**

102

The fattest troll lurches over and peers down at you saying, 'What are you? Are you wolves without fur? Are you orcs with hair? We're looking for food.'

The stench from the troll is overpowering and you have to swallow hard to prevent yourself from vomiting.

Chat? **Go to 123**

Attack? **Go to 94**

103

The forester looks amused, holds up a vial of cloudy elixir and asks, 'Do you wish to buy a bunch of freshly cut Sogweed?'

Ashto nods and says, 'Sogweed's a very powerful and poisonous plant, and rare, even in these parts. Very useful against giant swamp spiders, I understand.'

You'll need **15** groats to buy the Sogweed. If you buy the Sogweed, deduct **15** groats from your adventure sheet and add the elixir.

Attack? **Go to 158**

Leave? **Go to 98**

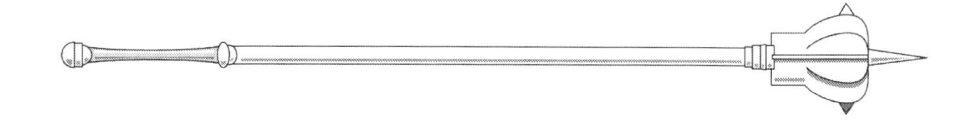

104

A vicious wind makes progress difficult. Snakes hiss in the undergrowth. Ashto mutters, 'I might come back for that plinth. I can get good money for that stone.'

Deduct **1** from your **Time** score. Out of time? **Go to 413**

Which way do you go next?

East? **Go to 247**
North? **Go to 256**
South? **Go to 26**

105

How will you open the chest?
Possess a silver key? **Go to 357**. Else, continue.

Turn Key 1?
Roll **1D6**
Roll 1 or 2? **Go to 185**
Roll 3 or 4? **Go to 249**
Roll 5 or 6? **Go to 153**

Turn Key 2?
Roll **1D6**
Roll 1 or 2? **Go to 249**
Roll 3 or 4? **Go to 153**
Roll 5 or 6? **Go to 185**

Turn Key 3?
Roll **1D6**
Roll 1 or 2? **Go to 153**
Roll 3 or 4? **Go to 185**
Roll 5 or 6? **Go to 249**

106

Roll **2D6**. How does this score compare to your **Charisma?**
Lower? **Go to 90**
Equal or higher? **Go to 55**

107

The clouds part and you're caught in a sudden burst of sunshine. This makes Ashto smile and he gives you a broad smile and starts whistling. If you've already killed the tinker, **go to 352**. If not, continue.

A tinker is strolling through the swamp. She's wearing a yellow cotton dress and skin-coloured tights, with a gorgeous white wide-brimmed harvest hat and a scruffy blue hessian cloak.

Ashto mutters, 'Tinkers are always cussing. Potty-mouthed, the lot of them!'

Avoid? **Go to 36**
Greet? **Go to 191**
Attack? **Go to 224**

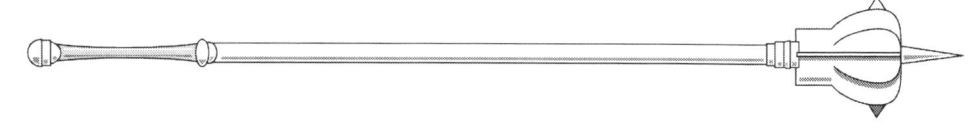

108

Test your **Dexterity**. Roll **2D6**. How does this score compare to your **Dexterity**?
Equal or higher? **Go to 1**
Lower? **Go to 315**

109
You successfully make your way across the chasm to the far side where you wait for Ashto to make his way across. **Go to 79**

110
The tinker grins as you approach and says happily, 'Hello there! Can I interest you in some of my wares? They're quite exquisite.'

Ashto glowers.

Buy? **Go to 198**
Leave? **Go to 176**
Attack? **Go to 258**

111
As you try to leave you get caught in a thick sticky strand of webbing which is coating all the surrounding undergrowth.
Greet? **Go to 18**
Attack? **Go to 387**

112
The goblins have spotted you! Roll **2D6**. How does this score compare to your **Charisma**?
Lower? **Go to 291**
Equal or higher? **Go to 175**

113

You feel as if you're being watched as you leave. Ashto is tugging at his beard. **Go to 87**

114

The sturdy and rusted iron chest stands on a heavily weathered and somewhat overgrown stone plinth. Arrayed along the front of the chest is a row of keys numbered one to three. An empty keyhole sits to their right and above each of the keys is a small iron nozzle. The chest seems designed to be opened, and who knows what may be inside?

Ashto pulls studiously on his beard and says, 'It seems you have to turn the keys in a specific order to trigger the opening mechanism. Or perhaps there's a master key that will fit the empty keyhole and enable you to open the chest.'

Examine? **Go to 316**
Leave? **Go to 170**
Attack? **Go to 353**

115

Among the goods the villages have abandoned as they flee their homes is an ancient and empty cart being pulled along by a remarkably skinny pair of oxen.

Jumping aboard you grab the reins and steer it away from the approaching Skeleton Horde. In the disorderly rout, several elderly villagers fall beneath the hooves of your oxen and their screams are terrible to behold as they perish beneath the hoods of our beasts.

Ashto screams, 'Get out of the way, you idiots! It's their own fault, they should have left days ago.'

You steer away path into the trees beyond the village and looking over your shoulder you see a red mist rise above Pigginmud as the Skeleton Horde descend upon the defenceless villagers.

Which way do you steer?

Left? **Go to 183**
Right? **Go to 376**
Straight ahead? **Go to 411**

116

The least underfed brigand points west into the swamp and rasps, 'Are you another seeking the Goblet of doom? It might be that way, but the Cave of Nak is a dangerous and cursed place and is to be avoided. And beware the wooden faun!'

Leave? **Go to 82**
Attack? **Go to 202**

117

You stand on the green circular flagstone and pray to the gods to let you pass. Test your **Charisma**. Roll **2D6**. How does this score compare to your **Charisma**?

Equal or higher? **Go to 109**
Lower? **Go to 79**

118

The minstrel doesn't see you and as you carry on your journey Ashto kicks a loose stone along the ground. **Go to 67**

119

The witch sniggers and says, 'Do you want a hex of Knowledge? A hex of Power or a hex of Time?'

Ashto strokes his beard and says, 'Hmmm! All very useful!'

You may buy one or none of the following items and adjust your number of groats accordingly.
(You may refer to the Spell chart at the front of this volume if you're not sure what each spell does.)

Hex of Knowledge = **15** groats

Hex of Power = **15** groats

Hex of Time = **20** groats

When you're ready, decide what to do next.

Attack? **Go to 334**

Leave? **Go to 137**

120

You carry on your journey wondering about the chest and who or what left it there.

Ashto pulls angrily at this beard and growls, 'Mysterious chests abandoned in swamps are a lottery of fortune, good and bad. Curse them!'

Deduct **1** from your **Time** score. Out of time? **Go to 413**

Which way do you go next?
East? **Go to 107**
West? **Go to 99**
North? **Go to 107**

121

Ashto grunts, 'I don't like foresters.'
Deduct **1** from your **Time** score. Out of time? **Go to 413**
Which way do you go next?
West? **Go to 33**
East? **Go to 43**
North? **Go to 48**

122

You stomp along the half-sunk path and the clusters of red maple and aspen trees give way to white oaks, elms and black willows. The breeze carries a faint trace of honey, a welcome change from the swamp's overpowering smell of rotting eggs. If you've already killed the forester, **go to 98**. If not, continue.

Marching through the swamp is a forester. Ashto grumbles, 'Foresters are tiresome sorts. Always chopping this and hewing that. Very limited people.'
Avoid? **Go to 320**
Greet? **Go to 302**
Attack? **Go to 158**

123

The stumpiest swamp troll chuckles and then growls, 'Food? Food! You are the food!' **Go to 94**

124

Ashto grins and says, 'An excellent decision! I can get a very good price for that in Tickstab, no questions asked! Have you ever been to Tickscab? The Fleeced Patron is a most forgiving tavern with the most potent ales. We shall do well there, with my wits and your brawn.'

How do you escape?
Abandoned cart? **Go to 115**
On foot? **Go to 200**

125

You step into the fiery portal and are immediately consumed by demonic flames and feel a strange dilation as if you're travelling through time. **Go to 10**

126

A large animal crashes through the reeds and birch trees to your right. You immediately duck into some tall bullrushes to your left to hide and then use them as cover to put some distance between yourselves and whatever the beast is.

After some time crawling through the stinking swamp mud, you emerge into a shaded dell, where a statue of a faun stands. It's created out of many pieces of wood nailed together and is easily over ten feet tall. The faun statue holds a longsword above its head, and the other hand is outstretched and open as if waiting to receive a gift.

Ashto yawns, 'This is obviously a spirit of very powerful magic, and we must pay homage in order to be judged worthy of receiving a gift. No doubt a spirit will be along shortly to explain this all to us.'

Avoid? **Go to 30**
Greet? **Go to 210**
Attack? **Go to 190**

127

The brigands don't see you and you carry on your journey and Ashto breathes a sigh of relief. **Go to 82**

128

The witch stomps over to you and taps your chest with her broomstick, 'What do you want? Why are you in this swamp? Hunting? Foraging? Are you lost?'

Chat? **Go to 60**
Attack? **Go to 334**

129

The rain that has been blowing in your face for the last half an hour, turning colder and colder until you're now struggling through a moving wall of sleet. Then suddenly the wind drops, the rain ceases and a bright sunshine floods the swamp. Immediately clouds of flying insects appear and start to bite you. You hurry along the path and try to outpace them.

A tinker is strolling through the swamp. She's wearing a yellow cotton dress and skin-coloured tights, with a gorgeous white wide-brimmed harvest hat and a scruffy blue hessian cloak.

Ashto mumbles something about not trusting tinkers.

Avoid? **Go to 396**
Greet? **Go to 110**
Attack? **Go to 258**

130

Test your **Dexterity**. Roll **2D6**. How does this score compare to your **Dexterity**?

Equal or higher? **Go to 51**
Lower? **Go to 77**

131

You tentatively step out onto the bridge and slowly make your way across the chasm to the other side.

Ashto punches your back and cries, 'I told you that bridge was safe! There's nothing more reliable than dwarf construction! Or an honest dwarf!' **Go to 79**

132

The orcs see you and surround you, preventing you from escaping by levelling their bloodied swords at you. The sweatiest orc

knocks you to the ground.
Confess? **Go to 254**
Attack? **Go to 50**

133

The path is dry and you make good progress among the cottonwood and ash trees. Large reeds, taller your head, lean over and allow the occasional small spider to fall on you.

Frogs croak as herons glide overhead. You're almost enjoying yourself when Ashto grabs your shoulder and points through the swamp to a nearby clearing where a brigand sits, cleaning a knife.

Ashto grumbles, 'Never trust anyone wearing an all-green outfit by choice. It makes one resemble an oversized leprechaun. And you can never trust leprechauns. Devious creatures.'

Avoid? **Go to 177**
Greet? **Go to 45**
Attack? **Go to 135**

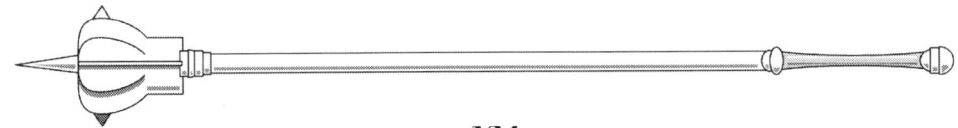

134

Test your **Dexterity**. Roll **2D6**. How does this compare to your **Dexterity**?
Equal or higher? **Go to 308**
Lower? **Go to 118**

135

The brigand is angered by your hostility but is quick to defend herself. Ashto takes cover behind a tree. Fight!

Brigand

Initial attack score: **11**

Weapon damage: **3**

Strength: **6**

Lose? **Play again!** Win? **Go to 335**

136

The door won't open and the poison gas is beginning to overwhelm you. Deduct **1D6** from your **Strength** score.

Dead? **Play again!**

Alive? Ashto can barely breathe and is slumped against the wall with a resentful look on his face. Although it's agony to breathe you take another gulp of air and bend down to try to lift the door.

Test your **Strength**. Roll **4D6**. How does this score compare to your **Strength**?

Equal or higher? **Go to 398**

Lower? **Go to 238**

137

The clouds darken and a spot of rain falls down the back of your collar sending shivers down your spine as you continue your journey.

Ashto mutters, 'I told you, witches aren't anything but trouble.'

Deduct **1** from your **Time** score. Out of time? **Go to 413**

Which way do you go next?
South? **Go to 68**
West? **Go to 63**
East? **Go to 53**

138

You pass quickly through the portal and arrive unharmed in a large cool stone chamber.

Ashto sticks his thumbs in his belt and declares, 'See! I told you I'm the clever one in this operation! What would you do without me?' Deduct **1** from your **Time** score. Out of time? **Go to 413**
Alive? **Go to 184**

139

A mysterious force prevents you from leaving the plinth.
Go to 301

140

You move carefully past the sundial. Ashto eyes it suspiciously.
Go to 41

141

The tinker doesn't see you and as you carry on your journey Ashto breathes a sign of relief. **Go to 176**

WITCH

142

The witch strides over to you and smacks your chest with her broomstick, 'What do you want? Why are you in this swamp? Looting? Burning? Are you mad?'

Chat? **Go to 181**
Attack? **Go to 388**

143

The wizard laughs and says, 'Never strike a wizard!' And he throws up his right hand as if about to conjure a spell. And as you're hypnotised by his movement his staff sweeps around in a fluid arc and smites you accurately on the skull, verily but hard. Deduct **1** from your **Strength** score. Dead? **Play again!**

Alive? Then the wizard disappears in a puff of green smoke. Ashto regards you with scant regard. **Go to 260**

144

Ashto pulls at his beard and grumbles, 'Time is fast and we are not! We must make speed!' Deduct **1** from your **Time** score. Out of time? **Go to 413**. Which way do you go next?

South? **Go to 146**
North? **Go to 126**
West? **Go to 122**

145

Choose either an apple, an orange or a banana to pluck.
Test your **Dexterity**. Roll **2D6**. Is this score higher, lower or equal to your **Dexterity**?
Higher? **Go to 295**
Equal? **Go to 304**
Lower? **Go to 250**

146

Have you obtained the Goblet of Zakzak already?
Yes? **Go to 261**
No? **Go to 10**

147

The path you're following has become little more than a wide smelly trough that you must negotiate while dodging low-hanging branches. Sandpipers flit about as you trudge through the ankle-deep muddy, stinking water.

Ashto grabs your elbow and turns you to the left and points through the swamp where a gang of goblins are scuttling through the swamp.

Ashto moans, 'I hate those dirty creatures!'
Avoid? **Go to 365**
Greet? **Go to 371**
Attack? **Go to 317**

148

The minstrel swings their lute as a makeshift club! Ashto pretends to be a tender birch tree. Fight!
The Minstrel
Initial attack score: **7**
Weapon damage: **2**
Strength: **4**
Lose? **Play again!** Win? **Go to 78**

149

You cast the Hex of Drawing and a deafening clanking sound echoes about the cavern as the enormous drawbridge slowly lowers itself on its enormous rusted chains. With a reverberating clang, the drawbridge lands on the stone edge of the chasm near your feet kicking up a cloud of dust and particles. Although built of thick oak beams trussed with iron bars, the wood is dark and twisted with age, and the iron is thin and mottled by long centuries of use.

Ashto twists his beard, 'This bridge must have been built by dwarves, look at the craftsmanship! It's as trustworthy as I am, I'd wager!'
Bridge? **Go to 131**
Rope? **Go to 49**
Plank? **Go to 58**

150

The tinker swings her bag on a stick off her shoulder and untying the spotted bag, opens it on the grass to show off their wares. You may buy one or none of the following items and adjust your number of groats accordingly.

Ashto grins and says, 'Red wine is most medicinal!'
A bottle of red wine (Worth **4** alcohol rations) = **12** groats
A lute = **30** groats
A jar of Howlmeat = **10** groats

When you're ready decide what to do next.
Leave? **Go to 352**
Attack? **Go to 224**

151

You feel as if you're being watched as you leave. Ashto is pulling at his beard. **Go to 343**

152

Remove one groat from our adventure sheet. You examine the sundial carefully and eventually decide which slot to drop the groat into. Ashto watches you intently.

Roll **2D6**. How does this score compare to your **Dexterity** score?
Lower? **Go to 22**
Equal or higher? **Go to 168**

153

There's a sharp click! A tiny dart flies out of the lock mechanism and stings you. Deduct **1D6** from your **Strength** score.
Dead? **Play again!** Alive? Ashto regards you with maximum scorn.
Go to 120

154

Ashto scratches at his beard and groans, 'Time is capricious! We must up our tempo!'
Deduct **1** from your **Time** score. Out of time? **Go to 413**
Which way do you go next?
South? **Go to 266**
East? **Go to 282**
North? **Go to 275**

155

Test your **Dexterity**. Roll **2D6**. How does this compare to your **Dexterity** score?
Equal or higher? **Go to 179**
Lower? **Go to 235**

156

You enter the next passageway and after some crawling by torchlight through a cramped and damp tunnel, the floor of which grazes your knees and elbows, you finally emerge into a small square cavern and gratefully stand up.

The air is stale and acrid but not as fetid as in previous caves and the walls are smooth and polished to match the smartly tiled floor. In the wall next to a stout ironbound wooden door is a small hexagonal hole about the width of a broom handle. Set in the walls at floor level are a series of closed metal grills.

As you cross the room to investigate a second door slams shut behind you, cutting off your exit and sealing you in this chamber.

Ashto groans loudly and mutters, 'This is a disappointingly basic method of protection. One must open the proceeding door before we're poisoned or perhaps drowned by whatever liquid or gas issues forth from those grills.'

Suddenly the metal grills slide open and a yellow smoke begins to drift into the room and Ashto shrieks, 'Aah, poison smoke. I was correct!'

Lift? **Go to 398**
Hex of Clouds? **Go to 160**
Winch? **Go to 251**

157

The giant swamp spider screeches as it skitters towards you on its thick hairy legs. As it approaches you discover their stench is almost overpowering in its toxicity. The spider chitters, 'You smell tasty!'

Chat? **Go to 106**
Attack? **Go to 55**

158

The forester heaves their axe and flexes their huge muscles. Ashto faints.

Forester

Initial attack score: **14**
Weapon damage: **8**
Strength: **16**
Lose? **Play again!** Win? **Go to 196**

159

Suddenly the air begins to warm and from a shimmering green haze a fairy appears. Piles of ragged hair fall over his translucent skin and across his sparkling knee-length tunic made of leaves.

Ashto grins, 'I told you so.'

The fairy bows and says, 'Hello and listen carefully for the faun of the swamp is impatient and capricious. There's no gift without pleasure, no weapon without treasure, pay homage to the great faun, or witness no dawn.'

Homage costs **1** groat. If you want to pay homage you must have at least **1** groat. If so, deduct one groat from your adventure sheet and go to that section.

Homage? **Go to 392**
Leave? **Go to 20**
Attack? **Go to 73**

MINSTREL

160

If you don't possess a Hex of Clouds, **go to 398**. If you do then continue.

You cast the Hex of Clouds and the poisonous smoke is sucked back into the grills and the door rises to allow you to continue. You turn and grin at Ashto who leans against the wall, performatively thumping his chest and coughing loudly.

Remove the Hex from your adventure sheet.

As the dwarf coughs and splutters to his heart's content, you head through the open doorway, leaving Ashto to hurry after you. Once in the next chamber, you see a large wooden handle.

Do you pull the handle up or down?

Up! **Go to 300**

Down! **Go to 189**

161

The cog turns quietly and you smile at having made the correct choice! But looking up to the ceiling instead of seeing the goblet being lowered, a steel blade is hurtling towards you!

Deduct **1D6 + 1** from your **Strength** score. Dead? **Play again!**

Alive? Ashto pulls frantically at his beard and cries, 'Not that one! The other cog! The other cog! Are you stupid?'

Your life may depend on this next decision. Which cog do you turn?

Cog 1? **Go to 213**
Cog 2? **Go to 83**
Cog 3? **Go to 46**
Cog 5? **Go to 239**
Cog 6? **Go to 311**
Cog 7? **Go to 246**
Cog 8? **Go to 323**
Cog 9? **Go to 285**

162

The forester swings their axe a few times, causing their enormous muscles to flex and bulge. Ashto collapses into a whimpering wreck.

Forester
Initial attack score: **14**
Weapon damage: **8**
Strength: **16**
Lose? **Play again!** Win? **Go to 406**

163

The minstrel has spotted you! Ashto moans.
Greet? **Go to 278**
Attack? **Go to 271**

164

Test your **Dexterity**. Roll **2D6**. How does this score compare to your **Dexterity**?
Equal or higher? **Go to 281**
Lower? **Go to 151**

165

You hurry past the fruit tree. Ashto tries to snatch an apple as you hurry past but misses. **Go to 324**

166

Ashto wags a finger at you and declares, 'Poison gas isn't the worst danger you'll find underground. Rockfalls are far more dangerous. And don't get me started on dragons. And Balrogs.'
Deduct **1** from your **Time** score. Out of time? **Go to 413**
Otherwise: **Go to 171**

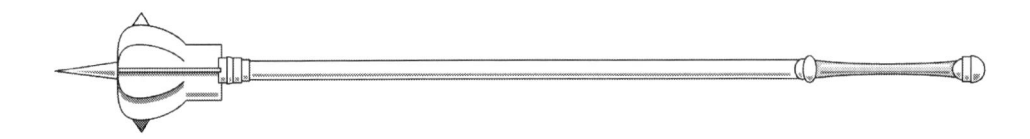

167

The forester is dressed in a brown tunic made of heavy leather, punctuated with iron studs. A heavy belt holds a sheathed knife and a cap is pulled down low over his face.

The forester stops, rests on his enormous double-headed axe and beckons you forward. He growls, 'What are you two idiots doing in this wretched place?'

Ashto moves to cower behind you.

Chat? **Go to 97**
Leave? **Go to 121**
Attack? **Go to 51**

168

The clouds begin to race past at an unnatural speed and you're overcome by waves of nausea which cause you to collapse to the ground. Ashto writhes on the ground next to you.

Roll **1D6** and deduct the result from your **Strength**. Deduct **1** from your **Time** score. Out of time? **Go to 413**
Otherwise: **Go to 29**

169

Ashto scratches his beard and mumbles, 'The only good giant swamp spider is a non-existent giant swamp spider.'

You search the spiders for spoils of combat and may take one of the following items:

A dead dormouse

A brass key

A packet of breadcrumbs (Worth **1** ration)

Go to 59

170

You carry on your journey wondering about the chest and who or what left it there.

Ashto pulls angrily at этого beard and growls, 'I like a chest full of groats as much as the next dwarf but there's something damnably outrageous about that one. Curse it!'

Deduct **1** from your **Time** score. Out of time? **Go to 413**
Which way do you go next?
East? **Go to 256**
South? **Go to 26**
West? **Go to 247**

171

You wander through tunnel after tunnel until you emerge into a torchlit chamber. As a heavy stone door slams down behind you, a stone lectern with a large book resting on it appears before you, at the same instant a portal of green fire erupts at the far end of the room.

Set on the stone floor before the lectern is a green circular flagstone which Ashto carefully avoids standing on as he goes to inspect the lectern. He spends a few moments scrutinising the ancient leather-bound tome and then turns to you and announces, 'Written on this page in ancient common runes are three spells of passing, one of which allows the educated to enter the inner sanctum without harm.'

Ashto gestures to the green circular flagstone and continues 'It's obvious one must stand on that stone and call out your chosen incantation, and then hurry through the portal before it closes. I'm by far the cleverest here. This shall be simplicity itself for a learned scribe such as myself!'

Yourself? **Go to 267**
Ashto? **Go to 193**
Portal? **Go to 401**

172

Ashto is carrying a leafy branch as a disguise as you leave the trolls behind you. **Go to 400**

173

The forester ignores you and carries on their journey. Ashto is sitting on the ground and panting heavily. **Go to 54**

174

Test your **Dexterity**. Roll **2D6**. How does this score compare to your **Dexterity**?

Equal or higher? **Go to 34**
Lower? **Go to 127**

175

The goblins are warriors and are always ready for a ruckus. Ashto farts with great nervousness.

Fight each goblin scout in turn! They're armed with evil-looking daggers. If you have a vial of Griffdum you can throw it at one goblin and it will kill them instantly. Don't forget to remove the vial from your adventure sheet.

As soon as you kill the first goblin you may pick up and use their weapon if you wish. Remember to write it down on your adventure sheet.

Goblin 1
Initial attack score: **7**
Weapon damage: **3**
Strength: **6**
Goblin 2
Initial attack score: **8**
Weapon damage: **3**
Strength: **7**
Goblin 3
Initial attack score: **9**
Weapon damage: **3**
Strength: **8**
Lose? **Play again!** Win? **Go to 61**

176

Ashto pulls at his beard and grumbles, 'Time is slipping! We must get hectic!'

Deduct **1** from your **Time** score. Out of time? **Go to 413**
Which way do you go next?
South? **Go to 21**
East? **Go to 23**
North? **Go to 29**

177

Test your dexterity. Roll **2D6**. How does this score compare to your **Dexterity**?

Equal or higher? **Go to 32**

Lower? **Go to 92**

178

You step into the fiery portal and are immediately consumed by demonic flames. You feel a strange dilation as if you're travelling through time. **Go to 10**

179

The goblins have spotted you! Test your **Charisma**. Roll **2D6**. How does this score compare to your **Charisma**?

Lower? **Go to 62**

Equal or higher? **Go to 349**

180

The most bloated and fetid spider waves a gnarly leg at you and chirrups, 'There are many orcs in the swamp, there's so many we can't catch them all. Orcs are tasty, much more than those vermin goblins.

Those goblins are too rancid to make a meal, not like nice plump dwarves.'

Attack? **Go to 387**

Leave? **Go to 11**

181

The witch raps your bicep with her broomstick and cries, 'Speak now! Do you want to buy a hex?'

You'll need a minimum of **20** groats to buy a hex.

Buy? **Go to 222**

Attack? **Go to 388**

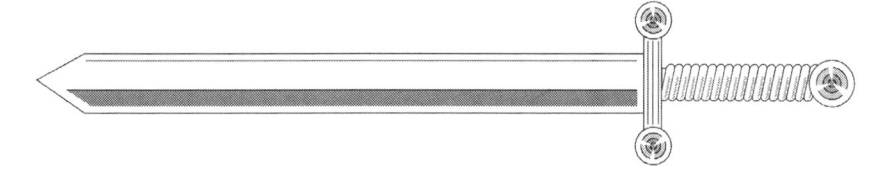

182

Ashto groans as you grasp the fruit but the fruit gods are in a mischievous fettle! Grasping the fruit feels like putting your hand in a furnace! Deduct **1** from your **Strength** score. Dead? **Play again!** Alive?

Pluck? **Go to 227**

Leave? **Go to 408**

Attack? **Go to 242**

183

You're ambushed by an orc warrior. As you begin defending yourself Ashto runs off into the trees and disappears. Fight!

COGS

Orc warrior

Initial attack score: **14**

Weapon damage: **9**

Strength: **9**

Lose? **Play again!** Win? **Go to 9**

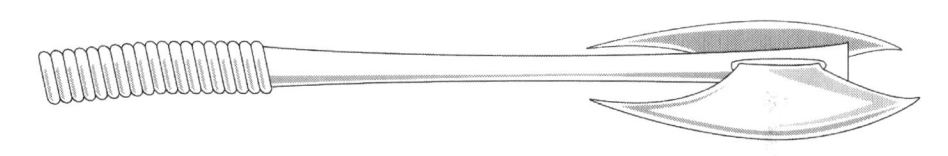

184

Suspended by silver thread from the carved stone ceiling hangs the fabled Goblet of Zakzak!

Blades project from thin rectangular holes in the ceiling. Flaming torches stand at regular intervals at the edge of the chamber and their light causes the exceedingly sharp-looking blades to glint.

There are a hundred such holes in the ceiling and they're so positioned that if the blades were to fire there's no place inside the chamber where anyone would be safe. Beneath the goblet stands a dwarf-high nine-sided stone pedestal, decorated with nine iron cogs.

Ashto pulls on his beard and declares, 'Ah yes, the pedestal of the nine gods! You must turn the correct cog to withdraw the blades and release the goblet! I'm sure you'll choose wisely.' And with that Ashto sidles to the edge of the room and tries to make himself as thin as possible against the wall, to best avoid any blades that may be fired at anyone careless enough to turn the wrong cog.

Your life may depend on this next decision. Which cog do you turn?

Cog 1? **Go to 213**
Cog 2? **Go to 83**
Cog 3? **Go to 46**
Cog 4? **Go to 161**
Cog 5? **Go to 239**
Cog 6? **Go to 311**
Cog 7? **Go to 246**
Cog 8? **Go to 323**
Cog 9? **Go to 285**

185

There's a sharp click! A tiny dart flies out of the lock mechanism and stings you. Ashto regards you with sneering disgust. Deduct **1D6** from your **Strength** score. Dead? **Play again!**
Alive? **Go to 120**

186

Test your **Dexterity**. Roll **2D6**. How does this score compare to your **Dexterity**?
Equal or higher? **Go to 73**
Lower? **Go to 214**

187

The emerald fairy smiles and says, 'You have been judged faithful to the eternal faun. Now prepare yourself for your reward.'

Ashto's eyes light up as three strong wooden green chests appear on the grass before you.

Make your choice. You may take one or none of the following:
A small jar of Howlmeat
A **FLAIL**
A length of rope
Go to 87

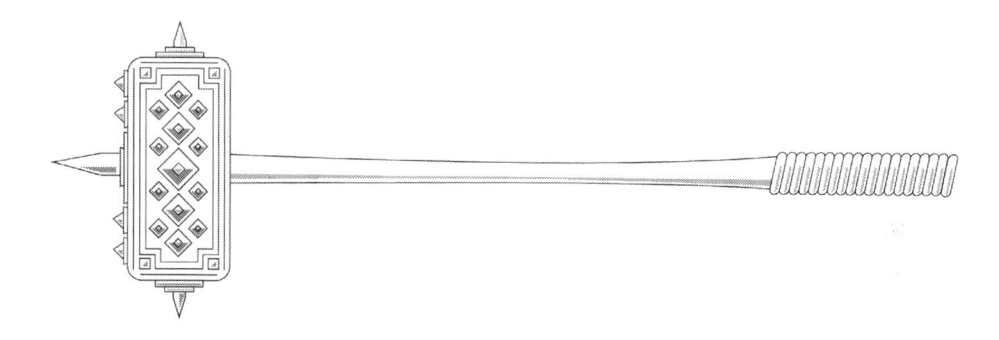

188

The nearest troll swings at you with a war hammer! Ashto crouches down and pretends to be a rock, casually placed there via a process of glaciation many millennia ago.

Fight each troll in turn! You may use Howlmeat if you have it. One jar of howlmeat is sufficient to poison one troll and kill it. Remember to deduct each jar of howlmeat from your adventure sheet as you use it. As soon as you kill the first troll you may pick up their war hammer and use it in combat. Remember to write it on your adventure sheet.

Swamp troll 1

Initial attack score: **12**

Weapon damage: **11**

Strength: **21**

Swamp troll 2

Initial attack score: **13**

Weapon damage: **11**

Strength: **20**

Swamp troll 3

Initial attack score: **14**

Weapon damage: **11**

Strength: **22**

Lose? **Play again!** Win? **Go to 340**

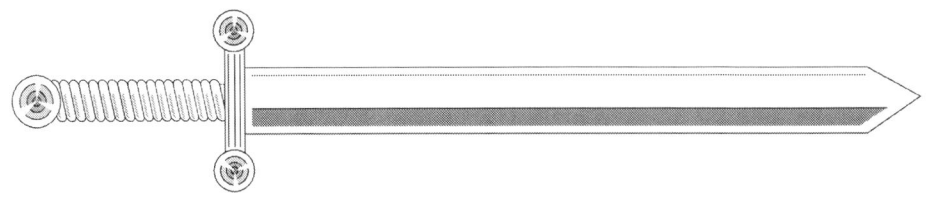

189

You pull down the lever. The door slams down behind you and you're safe from the poisonous gas. **Go to 166**

190

The wooden faun steps forward and attacks! Ashto pretends to be a shrub. Fight!

Wooden Faun

Initial attack score: **18**

Weapon damage: **12**

Strength: **6**

Lose? **Play again!** Win? **Go to 87**

191

The tinker grins as you approach and says happily, 'Hello there! Have we met before? And may I interest you in some of my wares? They're really quite exquisite.'

Ashto grumbles to themself.

You'll need a minimum of **10** groats to buy something.

Buy? **Go to 150**

Leave? **Go to 352**

Attack? **Go to 224**

192

The dirtiest goblin sniggers, 'You'll get no information from us, you! Be off with you before we summon the Poppy Scouts!'

Leave? **Go to 175**

Attack? **Go to 349**

193

Ashto steps steadily onto the green flagstone and with a booming voice recites a spell. The flames leap higher and you feel a dramatic increase in temperature on your skin.

And then with a deep breath, Ashto walks boldly into the portal of green fire. He passes seemingly unharmed and from the other side beckons you through. Do you follow Ashto into the searing flame?
Yes? **Go to 117**
No? Ashto grows bored waiting for you and wanders off through the green flame. The chamber is becoming increasingly hot.

Do you have a diamond ring to use as protection?
Yes? **Go to 125**
No? **Go to 178**

194

The brigand stands up and moves slowly forward with their hands firmly holding their dagger as they approach. Then the brigand looks you up and down and says, 'You're a long way from safety. This swamp isn't safe for the unwary.'
Chat? **Go to 355**
Leave? **Go to 330**
Attack? **Go to 262**

195

Ashto likes you. He's giddy with delight and performs a dwarfish victory jig around the pedestal, crying, 'I did it! I did it! All praise to Xullu, most majestic and merciful, the Most Major Miner, who dwells and digs in the Eternal Caverns! I did it! I did it!'

As you stuff the Goblet of Zakzak into your bag a mysterious blast of air blows out the flaming torches and you're plunged into darkness.

Add the Goblet of Zakzak to your adventure sheet. **Go to 261**

196

You search the forester and find three items. You can choose only one to take with you. You may take nothing if you wish.

Ashto groans, 'It was foolish to risk our lives for this! This!'
Make your choice:
A bunch of freshly cut Sogweed
An **AXE**
A small jar of Howlmeat
Go to 98

197

In a clearing to the left of your path stands an iron chest.
Avoid? **Go to 170**
Investigate? **Go to 114**
Attack? **Go to 353**

198

The tinker swings her spotted bag on a stick off her shoulder and after laying it on the grass, unties it and spreads out her wares.

You may buy one or none of the following items and adjust the number of groats on your adventure sheet accordingly.

Ashto grins and says, 'White wine is most medicinal!'
A bottle of white wine (Worth 5 alcohol rations) = **10** groats

A length of rope = **30** groats
A brass winch handle = **10** groats
When you're ready decide what to do next.
Leave? **Go to 176**
Attack? **Go to 258**

199

The faun raises its sword even higher! **Go to 281**

200

In your hurry to escape the incoming Skeleton Horde you push pregnant women and small children out of the way.

Ashto screams, 'Get out of the way, you idiots!'

You race away into the trees beyond the village. Looking over your shoulder you see a red mist rise above Pigginmud as the Skeleton Horde descends upon the defenceless villagers.

Ashto scowls, 'They should never have put their faith in a pair of mercenaries, should they? They've only themselves to blame. Still, We've achieved great deeds, great deeds indeed, my friend! Could you possibly be musing we should indulge in more lucrative exploits together?'

Which way do you go?
Left? **Go to 183**
Right? **Go to 411**
Straight ahead? **Go to 64**

WIZARD

201

The tinker has spotted you! Ashto groans.

Greet? **Go to 110**

Attack? **Go to 258**

202

The brigands are angered by your hostility and are quick to defend themselves. Ashto takes cover behind a tree.

Fight each brigand in turn.

Brigand 1

Initial attack score: **11**

Weapon damage: **9**

Strength: **6**

Brigand 2

Initial attack score: **13**

Weapon damage: **10**

Strength: **5**

Lose? **Play again!** Win? **Go to 57**

203

The key turns smoothly in the lock. At the bottom of the iron box a small hidden door flips open and spits groats at your feet. Before you can react the door snaps shut again. Roll **4D6** to determine how many groats you've received. **Go to 170**

204

The tinker has spotted you! Ashto groans.
Greet? **Go to 191**
Attack? **Go to 224**

205

There's a sharp click. A tiny dart flies out of the lock mechanism and stings you. Ashto regards you with undisguised contempt. Deduct **1D6** from your **Strength** score. Dead? **Play again!**
Alive? **Go to 170**

206

The goblins don't see you and you carry on your journey. Ashto stops to urinate behind a tree. **Go to 14**

207

You drop a groat into the stone slot and a bright green flame bursts from the nozzle on top of the plinth and you make swipe at it.

Test your **Dexterity**. Roll **2D6**. How does this score compare to your **Dexterity**?
Lower? **Go to 255**
Equal or higher? **Go to 310**

208

Heavy rain pours down, quickly flooding your path and turning the dry earth to thick mud. Dragonflies the size of your fist zip about and alligators can be heard thrashing through the reeds and grasses.

Between the oaks and elms, you glimpse a party of orcs. They're heavily armed and wearing the warpaint livery of the Bone Baron.

Ashto mutters, 'I loathe all orcs. We must annihilate them all. All of them. Do you hear me?'

Avoid? **Go to 326**
Greet? **Go to 329**
Attack? **Go to 50**

209

The brigand points south into the swamp and cries, 'That way lies the Goblet of Zakzak. But doom and disaster is all it brings! It is foretold! Beware the Goblet of Zakzak and beware the emerald fairy!'

Ashto rolls his eyes.

Leave? **Go to 144**
Attack? **Go to 135**

210

The air begins to warm and from a shimmering green haze a fairy appears. Piles of ragged hair fall over his translucent skin and across his sparkling knee-length tunic made of leaves.

Ashto shrugs, 'I told you so.'

The fairy bows and says, 'Hello and listen carefully for the faun of the swamp is impatient and capricious. There's no gift without pleasure, no weapon without treasure, pay homage to the great faun, or witness no dawn.'

Homage costs one groat. If you want to pay homage you must have at least one groat. If so, deduct one groat from your adventure sheet and go to that section.

Homage? **Go to 96**
Leave? **Go to 87**
Attack? **Go to 190**

211

The wizard rests on his staff and says, 'It feels like sunshine presently. I feel I've seen your clothes somewhere else. But then fashions are unfathomable to me. Time is passing and you're lost little lambs. Have you met our witch? Have I asked you that before? Living beyond the temporal realm can be so confusing. How may I help? Mind, a wizard's help is never without its price.'

Help? **Go to 91**
Leave? **Go to 56**
Attack? **Go to 143**

212

The minstrel strums their lute and sings you the rousing epic heroic tale of the famous orc slayer, Dingleberry the Hairy. At the end of the song you must decide what to do next.

Leave? **Go to 67**
Attack? **Go to 148**

213

Turning the cog is harder than you thought it would be but after a couple of tries it suddenly gives way and turns smoothly with a grinding noise. You see above you a sharp blade arrowing its way towards you from a hole in the ceiling.

Deduct **1D6** from your Strength score. Dead? **Play again!** Alive? Ashto is cowering at the edge of the room. Your life may depend on this next decision. Which cog do you turn?

Cog 2? **Go to 83**
Cog 3? **Go to 46**
Cog 4? **Go to 161**
Cog 5? **Go to 239**
Cog 6? **Go to 311**
Cog 7? **Go to 246**
Cog 8? **Go to 323**
Cog 9? **Go to 285**

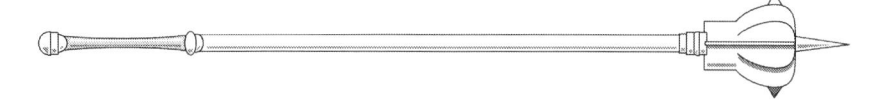

214

You feel as if you're being watched as you leave. Ashto is tugging at his beard. **Go to 20**

215

The witch has seen you! She extends a graceful hand and coyly beckons you to her. Ashto grins.

Chat? **Go to 181**

Attack? **Go to 388**

216

The rope catches in the hook and you test its weight before venturing out onto the plank and across the chasm, holding your flaming torch in your free hand.

Test your **Dexterity**. Roll **2D6**. How does this score compare to your **Dexterity**?

Equal or higher? **Go to 240**

Lower? **Go to 79**

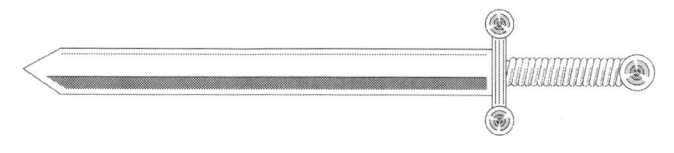

217

Test your **Dexterity**. Roll **2D6**. How does this score compare to your **Dexterity**?

Equal or higher? **Go to 390**

Lower? **Go to 234**

218

You search the tinker and find three items. You can choose only one to take with you.

Ashto grins and says, 'We should definitely take the white wine,

it's most soothing and good for one's bowels.'
Make your choice:
1 bottle of white wine (Worth **3** alcohol rations)
A length of rope
27 groats
When you're ready decide what to do next. **Go to 176**

219

The rain stops and a fine mist forms in its place. You're still wet through but the going is easier. The ground rises and the earth is a little firmer and less muddy. There seem to be more flowering plants here, and friendly bees are making themselves busy. Also, there seem to be fewer stinging insects mistaking you for a meal.

Ashto grabs your arm and twists you to the right. In a gap between the trees stands a nine-sided stone plinth. Ashto mutters, 'It's a crime to leave a decent bit of masonry like that lying about. Someone might have that away.'

Avoid? **Go to 263**
Investigate? **Go to 273**
Attack? **Go to 363**

220

The brigand doesn't see you and you carry on your journey. Ashto claps his hands with joy! **Go to 330**

221

The plinth is protected by a powerful magic spell and as you strike it you're repulsed by an invisible force which knocks you to the ground and leaves you shaken. Ashto wags a finger at you.

Roll **1D6** and deduct it from your **Strength** score.
Dead? **Play again!** Alive? You need at least **1** groat to pay tribute.
Leave? **Go to 5**
Tribute? **Go to 47**

222

The witch smiles and says, 'Do you want a hex of Knowledge? A hex of Power, or a hex of Time?'

Ashto strokes his beard and says, 'Hmmm! All very useful!' You may buy one or none of the following items and adjust your number of groats accordingly. (You may refer to the Spell chart at the front of this volume if you're not sure what each spell does.)
Hex of Knowledge = **20** groats
Hex of Power = **20** groats
Hex of Time = **30** groats
When you're ready, decide what to do next.
Attack? **Go to 388**
Leave? **Go to 274**

223

The faun raises its sword even higher! **Go to 190**

224

The tinker is startled but prepares to defend herself! Ashto farts nervously. Fight!

The Tinker
Initial attack score: **5**
Weapon damage: **1**
Strength: **3**
Lose? **Play again!** Win? **Go to 243**

225

A mysterious force prevents you from leaving the plinth.
Go to 273

226

The smelliest troll lumbers over and stares down at you saying, 'What are you? Are you cows without udders? Are you goblins with manners? We're looking for fire.'

The stink from the troll is overpowering and you have to swallow hard to prevent yourself from retching.

Chat? **Go to 241**
Attack? **Go to 188**

227

Choose either an apple, an orange or a banana to pluck. Test your **Dexterity**. Roll **2D6**.
Is this score higher, lower or equal to your **Dexterity**?

Higher? **Go to 37**
Equal? **Go to 8**
Lower? **Go to 182**

228

The emerald fairy smiles and says, 'You have been judged faithful to the eternal faun. Now prepare yourself for your reward.'

Ashto's eyes light up as three strong wooden green chests appear on the grass before you.

Make your choice. You may take one or none of the following:

A pair of sapphire earrings

An emerald bracelet

A diamond ring

Go to 343

229

You carry on your journey, and wonder how powerful the wizard is. Ashto pulls at this beard and growls, 'Wizards believe themselves better than ordinary mortals, what idiot would aspire to be one of them?'

Deduct **1** from your **Time** score. Out of time? **Go to 413**

Which way do you go next?

North? **Go to 312**

West? **Go to 289**

South? **Go to 393**

230

As you approach the Bone Baron, the Skeleton Horde forms a circle around you so that you can't escape.

The Bone Baron is ten feet tall and dressed head to toe in silver armour decorated with an intricate bone motif so that when the light glints it gives the appearance of her being a living steel skeleton.

Her helmet is shaped like a skull with enormous horns on either side, and she's armed with a majestic longsword.

Laughter comes from within the helmet and a voice says, 'Is this what's considered a champion in this land? What shall I do with your lifeless body? Shall I eat it? Leave it as a feast for the battlefield carrion? Or shall I raise it from the dead to serve me as a legionnaire in my undefeated Skeleton Horde, to do my bidding for all eternity?'

Fight! As the Bone Baron is wearing full body armour, after calculating your Damage Score, you must halve your Damage Score before deducting the score from the Bone Baron's Strength. However, if you win an Attack Round your Damage Score will always be a minimum of 1.

For example: if your Damage Score would normally be 12, in this combat it is only 6.

You may use Howlmeat if you have it. However, one jar of howlmeat is only sufficient to partially poison the Bone Baron. Reduce their Strength by half at any point. If you have two jars of howlmeat you can kill the Bone Baron outright. Remember to deduct each jar of howlmeat from your adventure sheet as you use it.

Fight!

The Bone Baron
Initial attack score: **24**
Weapon damage: **12**
Strength: **24**
Dead? **Play again!** Win? **Go to 410**

231

The wizard rests on his staff and says, 'It feels like sunshine presently. I feel I've seen your clothes somewhere else. Were you wearing it the last time we met? Time is inescapable and you're lost children without a friendly mentor to guide you. Have you met the witch? Have I asked you that already? Living beyond the temporal realm can be so discombobulating. How may I assist? Be warned, a wizard's help is never without penalty.'
Help? **Go to 307**
Leave? **Go to 287**
Attack? **Go to 383**

232

Ashto looks longingly over his shoulder at the luscious fruit as you hurry past the fruit tree. **Go to 397**

233

Red maple trees soar overhead as you trudge along a muddy path overgrown with spiky ferns and razor-sharp reeds. If you've already killed the forester, **go to 54**. If not, continue.

FORESTER

Hiking through the swamp is a forester. Ashto grumbles, 'Foresters are foolish types. Always felling this and hacking that. Very dull people.'
Avoid? **Go to 356**
Greet? **Go to 374**
Attack? **Go to 162**

234

Ashto dodges from tree to tree as you continue. **Go to 395**

235

The goblins don't see you and you carry on your journey. Ashto is leaning on a tree trunk and breathing hard. **Go to 407**

236

Test your **Dexterity**. Roll **2D6**. How does this compare to your **Dexterity** score?
Equal or higher? **Go to 163**
Lower? **Go to 305**

237

The orcs are highly trained fighting machines. And cruel with it. They don't know the meaning of the word 'surrender'. Or 'anachronistic'. Ashto pretends to faint and while lying on the ground he rolls away behind a nearby bush.

Fight each orc in turn. As soon as you kick the first orc you may pick up their shortsword and use it in combat. Don't forget to add it to your adventure sheet.

Orc warrior 1

Initial attack score: **14**

Weapon damage: **9**

Strength: **9**

Orc warrior 2

Initial attack score: **15**

Weapon damage: **9**

Strength: **10**

Orc warrior 3

Initial attack score: **16**

Weapon damage: **9**

Strength: **11**

Dead? **Play again!** Win? **Go to 369**

238

The door begins to rise and as soon as there's a sufficiently large gap to squeeze through, you climb beneath it and drag Ashto after you. Once in the next chamber, you see a large wooden handle. Do you pull the handle up or down?

Up! **Go to 300**

Down! **Go to 189**

239

The cog turns quietly and you smile at having made the correct choice. a silent prayer to the gods. Ashto stands up and straightens his beard as a hidden mechanism lowers the goblet to a height where you're able to release it from the silver thread. **Go to 195**

240

Your foot slips and you fall onto the plank with a crash. Deduct **1** from your **Strength** score. Dead? **Play again!** Alive? You slowly stand up. **Go to 412**

241

The smelliest swamp troll frowns and then chuckles, 'Fire? Fire to cook with! It's barbecue night tonight, and you're the meat for our grill!' **Go to 188**

242

You try to strike the tree but it's protected by a powerful magic spell which reverses your own power back at you. Ashto makes insulting hand gestures.

Deduct **1D6** from your **Strength** score. Dead? **Play again!** Alive? Chose what to do.
Pluck? **Go to 227**
Leave? **Go to 408**

243

You search the tinker and find three items. You can choose only one to take with you.

Ashto grins and says, 'Ale is most nourishing. A meal in a glass!' Make your choice:

Two bottles of ale (Worth **1** alcohol ration each)

A bar of soap

A jar of Sogweed

Go to 352

244

The forester has spotted you! Ashto squeals. **Go to 51**

245

The wizard casts a spell and your feet turn of their own accord and march you over to the wizard.

Greet? **Go to 211**

Attack? **Go to 143**

246

The cog is difficult to turn but eventually, you manage to get some traction and it slowly inches around. Deep within the pedestal, there's a low mechanical groan and you're suddenly struck by a steel blade fired from the ceiling. Deduct **3** from your **Strength** score. Dead? **Play again!**

Alive? Ashto scratches frantically at his beard and shouts, 'You're so stupid! A child could do this! And stop getting blood everywhere, you'll attract cannibals and ne'er-do-wells!'

Your life may depend on this next decision. Which cog do you

turn? Choose carefully.
Cog 1? **Go to 213**
Cog 2? **Go to 83**
Cog 3? **Go to 46**
Cog 4? **Go to 161**
Cog 5? **Go to 239**
Cog 6? **Go to 311**
Cog 8? **Go to 323**
Cog 9? **Go to 285**

247

Scuttling through the swamp is a nest of goblins. Ashto moans, 'I hate those filthy creatures!'
Avoid? **Go to 155**
Greet? **Go to 62**
Attack? **Go to 349**

248

The most warty orc scuttles over and grabs your neck, spits in your face and growls, 'I hope you've good reason to be trespassing on the Bone Baron's land?'
Confess? **Go to 298**
Attack? **Go to 378**

249

The key turns smoothly in the lock. At the bottom of the iron box a small hidden door flips open and spits groats at your feet. Before you can react the door snaps shut again. Roll **4D6** to determine how many grants you've received. **Go to 120**

250

You grasp the fruit but the fruit gods are in a mischievous fettle! Ashto laughs and points at you. Grasping the fruit feels like putting your hand in a furnace!

Deduct **2** from your **Strength** score. Dead? **Play again!**

Alive? What do you do?

Pluck? **Go to 145**
Leave? **Go to 324**
Attack? **Go to 80**

251

If you don't possess a brass winch handle **go to 398**. If you do then continue.

You jam the winch into the hexagonal hole and start to desperately crank the winch before you're overwhelmed by the poisonous fumes. Test your **Dexterity**. Roll **2D6**. How does this score compare to your **Dexterity**?

Equal or higher? **Go to 136**
Lower? **Go to 238**

252

The branches of the ancient tree are laden with ripe and succulent apples, oranges and bananas.
Pluck? **Go to 227**
Leave? **Go to 408**
Attack? **Go to 242**

253

Ashto scratches at his beard and shouts, 'Time is not our friend! We must get angry with time!'
Deduct **1** from your **Time** score. Out of time? **Go to 413**
Which way do you go next?
North? **Go to 247**
East? **Go to 107**
South? **Go to 43**

254

The orc laughs, 'Confess away, there's no one who cares what you have to say! There's nothing you can say we could possibly want to hear! You're lucky it's us that caught you and not the Poppy Scouts or the Mustard Infantry that found you! We'll just torture you a little before murdering you and eating you!' **Go to 50**

255

You catch the flame in your fist but feel no pain. Instead, the flame disappears and a **Dexterity** spell drops out of the plinth into one of the trays. Mark this on your adventure sheet.

Ashto nods approvingly and says, 'I never took you being the religious type.' **Go to 104**

256

A large beast roars as it splashes its way through the swamp. A second beast shrieks and whimpers and you realise the first creature has caught its prey. The sound of tearing flesh and cracking bones encourages you to make faster time along the path. The path winds past black oaks and red elms, and you emerge into a shaded dell.

A statue of a sword-wielding faun, created out of many pieces of wood, stands in the centre of the dell. Easily over ten feet tall, the faun's sword is pure steel. The faun's other hand is outstretched and open as if waiting to receive a gift.

Ashto yawns, 'This is obviously a spirit of very powerful magic, and we must pay homage in order to be judged worthy of receiving a gift. No doubt a spirit will be along shortly to explain this all to us. This is a very basic sort of enchanted grove.'

Avoid? **Go to 164**
Greet? **Go to 6**
Attack? **Go to 281**

257

You catch the flame in your fist but feel no pain. Instead, the flame disappears and a **Strength** spell drops out of the plinth into one of the trays. Mark this on your adventure sheet.

Ashto looks at you and says, 'I prefer push-ups to keep myself in peak physical condition.' And then mimes a chest-expanding exercise.
Go to 5

258

The tinker is startled by your aggressiveness but prepares to defend herself and raises her fists! Ashto tries to hide. Fight!
The Tinker
Initial attack score: **5**
Weapon damage: **1**
Strength: **3**
Lose? **Play again!** Win? **Go to 218**

259

Not many yards away a large beast thunders through the undergrowth. Ashto mutters, 'I reckon with a couple of strong guys and a strong cart I could have that plinth away.'
Deduct **1** from your **Time** score. Out of time? **Go to 413**
Which way do you go next?
East? **Go to 382**
West? **Go to 147**
South? **Go to 233**

260

You carry on your journey, and wonder how one is chosen to be a wizard. Ashto spits and says, 'Wizards are a breed apart, what fool would aspire to join their ranks?'

Deduct **1** from your **Time** score. Out of time? **Go to 413**

Which way do you go next?

South? **Go to 75**

East? **Go to 93**

North? **Go to 84**

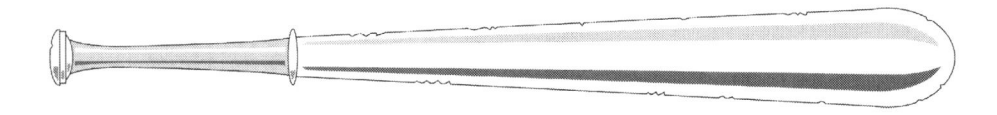

261

There's a blast of chilly air and a blinding flash of green light and you find yourselves stood outside the Cave of Nak.

Ashto sticks his thumbs in his belt and declares, 'See! I told you I'm the clever one in this operation! What would you do without me?'

You've succeeded in acquiring the goblet and now to accomplish your mission you must retrace your steps through the Swamp of Nok and take the goblet to Pigginmud. Even now the tyrannical Bone Baron and the Skeleton Horde are preparing to descend upon Pigginmud to murder and pillage.

Deduct **1** from your **Time** score. Out of time? **Go to 413**

North? **Go to 208**

East? **Go to 197**

South? **Go to 219**

262

The brigand is angered by your hostility but is quick to defend themselves. Ashto takes cover behind a tree. Fight!

Brigand 1
Initial attack score: **11**
Weapon damage: **3**
Strength: **6**
Lose? **Play again!** Win? **Go to 309**

263

Test your **Dexterity**. Roll **2D6**. How does this score compare to your **Dexterity**?
Equal or higher? **Go to 225**
Lower? **Go to 104**

264

The minstrel leans close to you in a conspiratorial manner and whispers, 'They say the Bone Baron can be defeated by filling the Goblet of Zakzak with red wine.'
What do you do next?
Leave? **Go to 399**
Attack? **Go to 347**

265

As you try to leave you get caught in a thick sticky strand

of webbing which is coating all the surrounding vegetation.
Greet? **Go to 364**
Attack? **Go to 409**

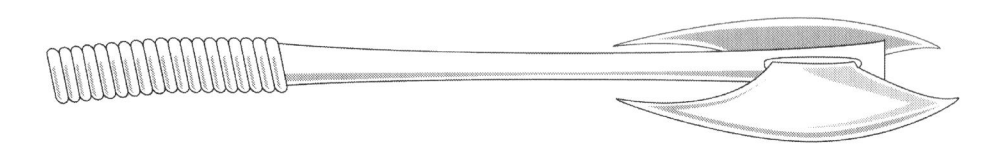

266

Heavy dark rainclouds gather overhead, rain begins to fall and soon you're soaked through. The filthy stinking swamp water rises and begins to wash over the tops of your boots.

You take shelter beneath the boughs of a majestic black oak tree. If you've already killed the wizard, **go to 229**. If not, continue.

A large puff of red smoke appears before you! When it clears a wizard is standing there, a minotaur, peering over half-moon spectacles as he tries not to fart. He's wearing a dark grey shirt with light grey trousers, a pair of tall black leather boots, a dark grey wide-brimmed hat with a tall point and a long flowing grey winter cloak.

Ashto mumbles, 'Wizards, pah! Just purveyors of party tricks for the simple of mind.'

Avoid? **Go to 101**
Greet? **Go to 231**
Attack? **Go to 383**

267

Brushing Ashto aside you study the runes written in the heavy

leather book and step onto the green portal. Can you read the common runes?
No? **Go to 117**
Yes? **Go to 19**

268

Test your **Dexterity**. Roll **2D6**. How does this score compare to your **Dexterity**?
Equal or higher? **Go to 55**
Lower? **Go to 2**

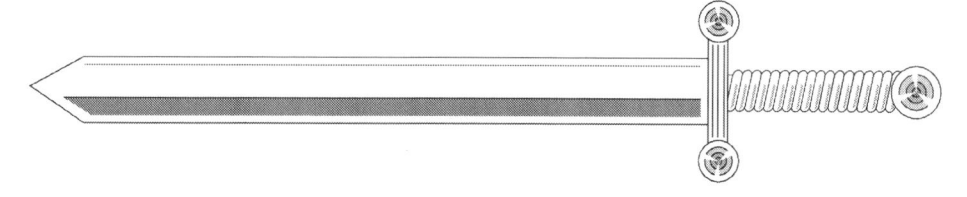

The forester doesn't see you and carries on their journey. Ashto is dabbing his brow with a handkerchief. **Go to 98**

270

Test your **Dexterity**. Roll **2D6**. How does this score compare to your **Dexterity**?
Equal or higher? **Go to 112**
Lower? **Go to 206**

271

The minstrel swings up their lute to use as a makeshift club! Ashto pretends to be a tree. Fight!

The Minstrel
Initial attack score: **8**
Weapon damage: **4**
Strength: **5**
Lose? **Play again!** Win? **Go to 288**

272

Ashto pulls at his beard and cries, 'Nothing good was ever found on an orc's corpse!'

You search the orcs for plunder and may take one of the following items:

A lockpick
A MACE
A silver key
Go to 405

273

Greatly overgrown and greatly weather-worn, the nine-sided stone plinth is waist-high to an average-sized adult halfling, and about halfway down each side there's a small iron nozzle pointing outwards.

Beneath each is a small stone tray to catch any objects deposited from a chute hidden within the plinth. On the top of the plinth is an inscription, beside which is a groat-sized slot and beside that, is a second smaller iron nozzle, blackened around the edges.

The inscription is written in the common runes and says, 'Pay tribute to the gods and challenge the odds. Catch the flame or suffer the pain.'

Ashto announces, 'Obviously what you must do is put a groat into the slot, and that activates a holy flame which the supplicant must grasp in their hand. The virtuous will be rewarded, and the sinners and undeserving will be punished. It's obviously a trap for the unworthy.'

If you want to pay tribute you must have at least **1** groat. If so, remember to deduct **1** groat from your adventure sheet.
Tribute? **Go to 207**
Leave? **Go to 104**
Attack? **Go to 363**

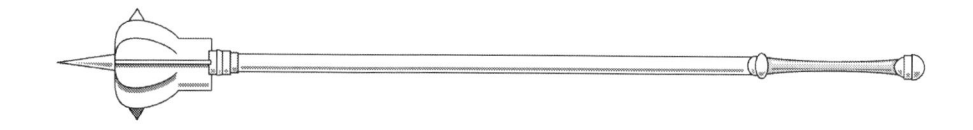

274

The clouds darken and you're suddenly covered in snow from a vicious and probably magical snowstorm which subsides almost as soon as it begins. You shake off the snow covering your head and continue your journey.

Ashto mutters, 'I told you, witches aren't anything but trouble. My but they're beautiful creatures though.'
Deduct **1** from your **Time** score. Out of time? **Go to 413**
Which way do you go next?

South? **Go to 322**
West? **Go to 332**
East? **Go to 342**

275

The path leads you between many magnificent black oaks and red maple trees. The ground between them is filled with reeds, rushes and flowering plants. And then sandwiched between two soaring oaks you discover a gnarly old fruit tree.

Ashto strokes his beard and mutters, 'This is clearly a tree of very powerful magic, some of the fruit will be wholesome and full of sustenance. Others will be less so, and possibly harmful. Maybe the swamp gods be merciful.'

Avoid? **Go to 165**
Investigate? **Go to 379**
Attack? **Go to 80**

276

You hand the Goblet of Zakzak to the sheriff and say, 'Take this for safekeeping, I'll save your village, and then maybe we'll reconsider my fee.' Remove the goblet from your adventure sheet.

The sheriff stashes the goblet in a leather satchel and says, 'Yes, yes, I'll keep it very safe.'

Ashto curses and says, 'I formally bring our partnership to an end! You're a lunatic, and I bid you farewell!' And the dwarf runs away.

The sheriff hands you a longsword and taking the formidable weapon, you stride forward to confront the Bone Baron! **Go to 230**

277

The plinth is protected by a powerful magic spell and as you strike it you're assaulted by an invisible force which smacks you to the ground and leaves you stunned. Ashto laughs and wags a finger at you. Roll **1D6** and deduct it from your **Strength** score.

Dead? **Play again!** Alive? What do you do? You need at least 1 groat to pay tribute. Remember to deduct it from your adventure sheet.

Leave? **Go to 259**
Tribute? **Go to 402**

278

The minstrel smiles cheerfully, and slaps you on the back before crying happily, 'Let the gods rejoice! I'm thrilled to meet you! For a small charitable donation, I shall share with you the gossip of the swamp to set you on your merry way!'

Ashto begins whistling tunelessly and tapping his foot.

If you wish to hear news of the swamp it will cost you **1** groat. Remember to deduct this from your adventure sheet.

News? **Go to 318**
Leave? **Go to 154**
Attack? **Go to 271**

279

The trolls have seen you and are pointing at you, rubbing their stomachs as they lurch over to your position.

Chat? **Go to 241**

Attack? **Go to 188**

280

You search the goblins and find three items. You can choose only one to take with you. Ashto groans, 'We risked our lives for this!'

Make your choice and remember to write it on your adventure sheet.

A half-eaten wooden chess pawn

A pair of six-sided dice

A dead stoat

Go to 407

281

The wooden faun steps forward and attacks! Ashto pretends to be invisible. Fight!

Wooden Faun

Initial attack score: **18**

Weapon damage: **12**

Strength: **6**

Lose? **Play again!** Win? **Go to 343**

282

A low mist turns into a thick fog and then turns into heavy rain. Ashto grunts, thumps your arm and points through the murk. Lurking among the trees and taking cover from the downpour is a brigand. Ashto mutters, 'Green? In this swamp? Brown would be more appropriate, don't you think?'
Avoid? **Go to 389**
Greet? **Go to 194**
Attack? **Go to 262**

283

The most sweaty orc jogs over and smashes you against a tree trunk and snarls, 'You're a pathetic excuse for a thief!'
Deny? **Go to 325**
Attack? **Go to 237**

284

You move carefully past the sundial. **Go to 391**

285

You turn the cog easily and hear a multitude of pneumatic devices firing at once. You're struck by several tiny blades fired from the ceiling. Deduct **2D6** from your **Strength** score. Dead? **Play again!**

Alive? Ashto looks up from his crouched position at the wall of the chamber and cries, 'Well hurry up and get on with it before we both get killed by your stupidity!'

Cog 1? **Go to 213**
Cog 2? **Go to 83**
Cog 3? **Go to 46**
Cog 4? **Go to 161**
Cog 5? **Go to 239**
Cog 6? **Go to 311**
Cog 7? **Go to 246**
Cog 8? **Go to 323**

286

Ashto is quietly cursing you as you sneak away from the orcs. Yet he is extremely careful not to draw attention to himself. **Go to 405**

287

As you walk away the wizards calls out, 'It's very unlucky to insult a wizard!' And you feel a tingling From the top of your head to the end of your toes as the wizard casts a hex on you.

Deduct **1** from your **Dexterity** score.

Deduct **4** from your **Charisma** score.

Deduct **2** from your **Strength** score.

Dead? **Play again!** Alive? Deduct **3** from your **Time** score. Out of time? **Go to 413**. Otherwise: **Go to 229**

288

You quickly search the minstrel and find three items. You can choose only one to take with you. Ashto chuckles and says, 'We should definitely take the loaf of dwarf bread, it's most nourishing!'

Make your choice and write it on your adventure sheet.

A loaf of dwarf bread (Worth **2** rations)

A lute, worn, rather battered and now missing three strings (Weapon score **4**, Damage score **4**. Still playable.)

7 groats

Go to 154

289

Thunder rolls and a moment later lightning forks across the sky. And then the rain begins. A heavy, persistent and dismal rain that seeps through your cloak and clothes, and freezes your bones.

Looking for somewhere to shelter you duck under the boughs of an ancient red maple, and across a clearing, you see a pack of bickering swamp trolls.

Each is enormous, the girth and height of a young oak tree. Though these trolls have seen many summers. Ashto mutters, 'I've heard many things about trolls. And none of them good.'

Avoid? **Go to 333**

Greet? **Go to 226**

Attack? **Go to 188**

290

The wizard casts a spell and your legs turn of their own volition and walk you over to the wizard.
Greet? **Go to 231**
Attack? **Go to 383**

291

The goblins change direction to scuttle towards you. Small, wiry, snaggletoothed and filthy, they're covered in rough tattoos indicating their allegiance to the Bone Baron.

The vilest one sniffs you and sniggers, 'Do you have your travel pass?'
Chat? **Go to 95**
Leave? **Go to 14**
Attack? **Go to 175**

292

Handing over the goblet, you explain you'll be leaving the village to its fate as soon as you've received the reward money for the goblet.

Remove the Goblet of Zakzak from your adventure sheet.

In reply, the sheriff spits at you and throws a leather bag full of groats at your feet.

Then the sheriff draws his sword, grits his teeth and sets off to rally whatever allies he can find among the fleeing populace.

Ashto grins, 'Quite right too. Now let's away with your loot!'

You scoop up the bag of cash before Ashto can reach it, and then you count it out.

Roll **2D6** and multiply by **6**. Then divide that number by **2** to account for Ashton's share and add this number of groats to your adventure sheet.

Ashto mutters, 'Is this it? Is that all we get for risking our lives? The ungrateful wretches. I hope the Bone Baron has their guts for breakfast!'

There are screams and suddenly the throng of villagers stop pushing past you and turn to race for the safety of the village, chased by the charging Skeleton Horde! Leading the charge is the Bone Baron!

Ashto screams, 'We must escape! I want no part of this fight! I want to spend my money, not be molested by the undead!'

How do you escape?
Abandoned cart? **Go to 377**
On foot? **Go to 25**

293

You step forward to the emerald fairy and hand over a groat, who smiles and bows and says, 'Are you a devout follower of the eternal faun? You are about to be tested. The faithless will be punished most severely but the rewards are rich for the devoted.'

Test your **Charisma**. Roll **2D6**. How does this score compare to your **Charisma**?
Lower? **Go to 228**
Equal or higher? **Go to 281**

294

The sturdy and rusted iron chest stands on a heavily weathered and somewhat overgrown stone plinth. Arrayed along the front of the chest is a row of keys numbered one to three. An empty keyhole sits to their right and above each key is a small iron nozzle. The chest seems designed to be opened and who knows what may be inside?

Ashto tugs thoughtfully on his beard and says, 'It seems you have to turn the keys in a specific order to trigger the opening mechanism. Or perhaps there's a master key that will fit the empty keyhole and enable you to open the chest.'

Examine? **Go to 105**
Leave? **Go to 120**
Attack? **Go to 299**

295

You grasp the fruit but the fruit gods are in a mischievous fettle! Ashto grins. Grasping the fruit feels like picking a fruit! You pluck the fruit and tuck it away for later. Add your chosen fruit to your adventure sheet. Each piece of fruit is worth **1** ration. **Go to 324**

296

The minstrel doesn't see you and as you carry on your journey Ashto plucks a leave from a tree and shreds it as he walks along, scattering pieces of foliage behind him. **Go to 399**

297

Ashto nods approvingly. You grasp the fruit but the fruit gods are in a mischievous fettle! Grasping the fruit feels like picking a fruit! You pluck the fruit and tuck it away for later. Add your chosen fruit to your adventure sheet. Each piece of fruit is worth **1 ration**. **Go to 397**

298

The orc laughs, 'There's nothing you can say we could possibly want to hear. The Bone Baron knows all! And they're preparing the Fenlands for invasion by the Viscount of Dragon Skye's Purple League and the Freak dragon. But the Freak Dragon is for tomorrow. Today my scimitar is ready to quench its thirst!'
Go to 378

299

You attack the chest but it's protected by a powerful magic spell which blasts you to the ground. Ashto regards you with absolute disdain. Deduct **1D6** from your **Strength** score.
Dead? **Play again!** Alive?
Investigate? **Go to 294**
Leave? **Go to 120**

300

Nothing happens and the poison gas billows through the gap under the door. Deduct **1** from your **Strength** score. Dead? **Play again!**

Alive? Ashto pulls the wooden handle down and as the door slams down protecting you from the gas he shoots you a filthy look of contempt. **Go to 166**

301

Greatly overgrown and weather-worn, the nine-sided stone plinth is waist-high to an average-sized adult halfling, and about halfway down each side there's a small iron nozzle pointing outwards.

Beneath each nozzle is a small stone tray designed to catch any objects deposited from a chute hidden within the plinth. On the top of the plinth is an inscription, beside which is a groat-sized slot and a second smaller iron nozzle, blackened around the edges.

The inscription is written in the common runes and says, "Pay tribute to the gods and challenge the odds. Catch the flame or suffer the pain."

Ashto announces, 'Obviously what you must do is put a groat into the slot and that activates a holy flame which the supplicant must grasp in their hand. The virtuous will be rewarded, and the sinners and undeserving will be punished. It's obviously a trap for the unworthy.'

If you want to pay tribute you must have at least **1** groat. If so, deduct **1** groat from your adventure sheet and go to that section.
Tribute? **Go to 402**
Leave? **Go to 259**
Attack? **Go to 277**

302

The forester rests on his enormous double-headed axe and beckons you forward. 'What are you two fools doing in my domain?' Ashto quivers behind you.
Chat? **Go to 103**
Leave? **Go to 98**
Attack? **Go to 158**

303

The stone sundial has a thin bronze shadow-casting arm at its centre and at each of the nine points of the circle is a groat-sized slot.

Ashto scrutinises the sundial and says, 'This is obviously a shrine to the gods of Time. We must pay homage to the gods by placing a groat in a slot of our choosing, and if the gods are feeling beneficent they may bless us with more time to accomplish our mission. I've studied sundials such as this and we stand to gain at least a dozen hours if we choose the correct section!'

You need at least **1** groat to play this game. Remember to deduct it from your adventure sheet.
Play? **Go to 328**
Leave? **Go to 391**
Attack? **Go to 362**

304

You grasp the fruit but the fruit gods are in a mischievous fettle. Ashto groans. Grasping the fruit feels like picking up an old sock.

Suddenly the fruit collapses into a soggy pulpy mess and maggots start crawling out of it! Deduct **1** from your **Charisma** score.

Pluck? **Go to 145**

Leave? **Go to 324**

Attack? **Go to 80**

305

The minstrel doesn't see you and as you carry on your journey Ashto kicks a loose stone along the ground. **Go to 154**

306

Ashto is cursing you quietly as you sneak away from the orcs. **Go to 319**

307

The wizard smiles and offers you the following. (The game will tell you when you may use these very specific spells.)

Spell of Scaleless = **10** groats

Spell of Obscure = **15** groats

Spell of Glossa = **20** groats

Ashto strokes his beard and muses, 'Hmm, these must be powerful spells or possibly a filthy conjurer's trick, I don't recognise any of these spells.'

You may buy **1** of the spells. Remember to add the spell to your adventure sheet and deduct the groats.

If you can't afford to buy a hex or you choose not to: **Go to 287**

Otherwise, decide what to do next.
Attack? **Go to 383**
Leave? **Go to 229**

308

The minstrel has spotted you. Ashto moans.
Greet? **Go to 370**
Attack? **Go to 148**

309

You search the brigand and find three items. You can choose only one to take with you.

Ashto peers at the times, 'Elf bread? Disgusting stuff!'
Make your choice and write it on your adventure sheet:
A bow and quiver with **5** arrows (Weapon score 7, Damage score 7)
(You can only use this **5** times unless you acquire more arrows)
A pointed green hat with a peacock feather in it
A loaf of elf bread (Worth **3** rations)
Go to 330

310

The flame disappears before you have the chance to catch it and a red jet of flame shoots out of the nearest nozzle on the side of the plinth and burns you! Ashto laughs at you.

Roll **1D6** and deduct it from your **Strength** score. **Go to 104**

311

The cog turns easily and silently and you smile at having made the correct choice! But there's a sharp click and you're struck by a steel blade ejected from the ceiling at a great velocity.
Deduct **1D6** from your **Strength** score.
Dead? **Play again!** Else, continue.

Ashto tears frantically at his beard and cries, 'You idiot! Have I taught you nothing? It's obviously not that one!'

Your life may depend on this next decision. Which cog do you turn?

Cog 1? **Go to 213**
Cog 2? **Go to 83**
Cog 3? **Go to 46**
Cog 4? **Go to 161**
Cog 5? **Go to 239**
Cog 7? **Go to 246**
Cog 8? **Go to 323**
Cog 9? **Go to 285**

312

If you've already killed the witch, **go to 274**. If not, continue. Walking towards you is a witch. She's wearing a dark grey cotton shirt, black breeches with a pair of brown leather boots and a matching dark grey bandana and cloak.

Ashto mutters, 'I knew a witch once. She was the most adorable thing.'
Avoid? **Go to 384**
Greet? **Go to 142**
Attack? **Go to 388**

313

The brigands stand up and move slowly forward with their hands loosely gripping their weapons as they approach.

As Ashto cowers the least ragged one sniffs and says, 'Hello stranger.'
Chat? **Go to 116**
Leave? **Go to 82**
Attack? **Go to 202**

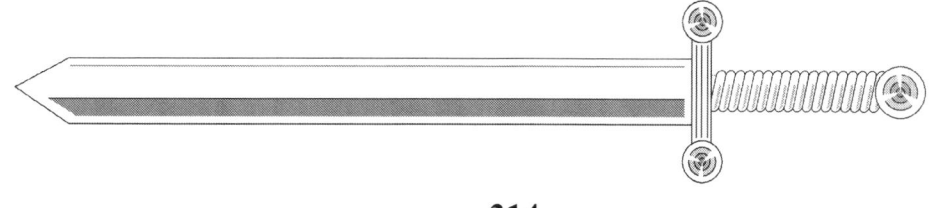

314

Ashto is trying not to snigger as you sneak away from the wizard. Add **1** to your **Charisma** score. **Go to 229**

315

Ashto is trying to appear as small as possible as you hurry away from the orcs. **Go to 12**

IRON CHEST

316

How will you open the chest?

If you possess a silver key? **Go to 3**

Else, choose a key to turn.

Turn Key 1?

Roll **1D6**

Roll 1 or 2? **Go to 205**

Roll 3 or 4? **Go to 203**

Roll 5 or 6? **Go to 394**

Turn Key 2?

Roll **1D6**

Roll 1 or 2? **Go to 394**

Roll 3 or 4? **Go to 205**

Roll 5 or 6? **Go to 203**

Turn Key 3?

Roll **1D6**

Roll 1 or 2? **Go to 394**

Roll 3 or 4? **Go to 203**

Roll 5 or 6? **Go to 205**

317

The goblins are warriors and are always ready for a ruckus. Ashto farts prodigiously.

Fight each goblin scout in turn. They're armed with evil-looking daggers. If you have a vial of Griffdum you can throw it at one goblin and it will kill them instantly. Don't forget to remove the vial from your adventure sheet. As soon as you kill one goblin you may add their dagger to your adventure sheet and use it in combat.

Goblin 1

Initial attack score: **7**

Weapon damage: **3**

Strength: **6**

Goblin 2

Initial attack score: **8**

Weapon damage: **3**

Strength: 7

Goblin 3

Initial attack score: **9**

Weapon damage: **3**

Strength: **8**

Lose? **Play again!** Win? **Go to 341**

318

The minstrel leans close to you in a conspiratorial manner and whispers, 'They say a brass winch handle is very useful in the Cave of Nak.'

Leave? **Go to 154**

Attack? **Go to 271**

319

You carry on your journey, wondering how many more orcs are wandering the land. Ashto curses and says, 'We must slaughter every orc we meet! Death and slaughter is what we oughta!'

Deduct **1** from your **Time** score. Out of time? **Go to 413**
Which way do you go next?
South? **Go to 247**
East? **Go to 336**
West? **Go to 275**

320

Test your **Dexterity**. Roll **2D6**. How does this compare to your **Dexterity** score?
Equal or higher? **Go to 158**
Lower? **Go to 269**

321

Roll **2D6**. How does this score compare to your **Charisma**?
Lower? **Go to 368**
Equal or higher? **Go to 409**

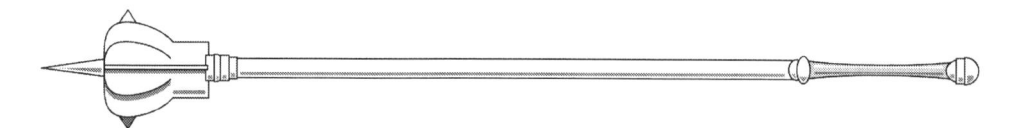

322

The wind howls about, whipping at the edges of your cloak which you pull tightly around you. The path curves to the left and on the right, among a bunch of tall, razor-sharp ferns, stands a gnarly old fruit tree. Ashto strokes his beard and mutters, 'This is clearly a tree of very powerful magic, some of the fruit will be wholesome and full of sustenance. Others will be less so, and possibly harmful. Maybe the

swamp gods be merciful.'
Avoid? **Go to 232**
Investigate? **Go to 381**
Attack? **Go to 344**

323

The cog turns more quickly than you expected and is accompanied by a mechanical grating noise. You're struck by a fast-flying steel blade fired from the ceiling.
Deduct **4** from your **Strength** score. Dead? **Play again!**

Alive? Ashto looks up and scratches uncontrollably at his beard, shouting, 'Curse you! Oh that I should be lumbered with such a numbskull!'

Your life may depend on this next decision. Which cog do you turn?

Cog 1? **Go to 213**
Cog 2? **Go to 83**
Cog 3? **Go to 46**
Cog 4? **Go to 161**
Cog 5? **Go to 239**
Cog 6? **Go to 311**
Cog 7? **Go to 246**
Cog 9? **Go to 285**

324

Ashto scratches at his beard and mutters, 'Make speed, make speed! Curse you and curse this swamp!'
Deduct **1** from your **Time** score. Out of time? **Go to 413**
Which way do you go next?
East? **Go to 289**
North? **Go to 393**
South? **Go to 312**

325

The orc laughs, 'I don't care if you're a thief or not! I'll tell you what you are, you're dinner!' **Go to 237**

326

Test your **Dexterity**. Roll **2D6**. How does this score compare to your **Dexterity**?
Equal or higher? **Go to 132**
Lower? **Go to 286**

327

The forester looks amused, holds up a vial of cloudy elixir and asks, 'Do you wish to buy a small jar of Howlmeat?'

Ashto says, 'That's a disgustingly pungent brew. Very useful against swamp trolls, I understand.'
If you buy the Howlmeat, deduct **15** groats from your adventure sheet and add the elixir.

Attack? **Go to 162**
Leave? **Go to 54**

328

Remove **1** groat from our adventure sheet. You examine the sundial carefully and decide which slot to drop the groat into.

Test your dexterity. Roll **2D6**. How does this compare to your **Dexterity**?
Lower? **Go to 345**
Equal or higher? **Go to 358**

329

The most meaty orc hikes over, knocks you to the ground with a single blow and growls, 'I hope you've good reason to be trespassing on the Bone Baron's land?'
Confess? **Go to 254**
Attack? **Go to 50**

330

Ashto yanks at his beard and mutters, 'Time is deserting us! We must hasten!'
Deduct **1** from your **Time** score. Out of time? **Go to 413**
Which way do you go next?
East? **Go to 289**
North? **Go to 393**
West? **Go to 312**

331

Ashto itches his beard and grunts, 'Evil beasts. Why you led me into a spider's nest I'll never fathom. Stupid person.'

You ransack the spiders for prizes of combat and may take one of the following items. Don't forget to add it to your adventure sheet.

A dead baby giant spider (Worth **1** ration)

A bronze key

A loaf of halfling bread (Worth **1** ration)

Go to 351

332

The dark clouds break and sunshine brightens the swamp. It even stops raining for a while and you manage to get reasonably dry. Even Ashto looks cheerful and has a jaunt in his step. If you've already killed the minstrel, **go to 399**. If not, carry on.

A minstrel is singing cheerfully and strumming a lute as they stroll through the swamp. A faun by species, she's wearing a frilly black silk shirt and skin-tight red leather trousers, with a scarlet wide-brimmed cavalier hat sporting a luxurious peacock feather and a long red silk scarf.

Ashto mumbles something about taking a hammer to the last lute he had the misfortune to encounter. And then Ashto mutters something about a wedding feast and that some people should have more of a sense of humour and not be so touchy. And that other people have strong

feelings too. Especially if they've forked out a lot of money for a present.
Avoid? **Go to 7**
Greet? **Go to 366**
Attack? **Go to 347**

333

Test your **Dexterity**. Roll **2D6**. How does this score compare to your **Dexterity**?
Equal or higher? **Go to 279**
Lower? **Go to 172**

334

The witch spins her broomstick around in her hands and adopts a fighting stance as the bristle-end of the broomstick snaps to a horizontal halt underneath one armpit and with the sharpened end pointing at you! Ashto closes his eyes. Fight!

Witch
Initial attack score: **14**
Weapon damage: **5**
Strength: **11**
Dead? **Play again!** Win? **Go to 137**

335

You search the brigand and find three items. You can choose only one to take with you. Remember to write it on your adventure sheet.

Ashto frowns and mutters something unsavoury and illegal about brigands.

Make your choice:

A bow and quiver with **3** arrows (Weapon score 7, Damage score 7) (You can only use this **3** times unless you acquire more arrows)

A pointed green hat with a peacock feather in it

A loaf of elf bread (Worth **3** rations)

Go to 144

336

You emerge from the swamp to see Pigginmud on the horizon. If you haven't found the Goblet of Zakzak then you must plunge back into the swamp to locate it. **Go to 336**.

If you have the goblet, continue.

You hurry to the village and eventually arrive on the village outskirts late in the day weighed down by the incredibly valuable and powerful Goblet of Zakzak.

The townsfolk are streaming past you, heading for safer territory and carrying whatever they can save from imminent destruction by the Skeleton Horde.

Keep? **Go to 124**

Deliver? **Go to 372**

337

The goblins have spotted you! Roll **2D6** and test your **Charisma**. How does this score compare to your **Charisma**?

Lower? **Go to 371**
Equal or higher? **Go to 317**

338

Test your **Dexterity**. Roll **2D6**. How does this score compare to your **Dexterity**?
Equal or higher? **Go to 71**
Lower? **Go to 5**

339

You search the minstrel and find three items. You can choose only one to take with you.

Ashto chuckles and says, 'We should definitely take the loaf of halfling bread, those little fellows are quite talented cooks.'
Make your choice:
A loaf of halfling bread (Worth **1** ration)
A lute, worn, rather battered and now missing three strings (Weapon score 4, Damage score 4)
3 groats
When you're ready decide what to do next.
Go to 399

340

Ashto pulls at his beard and cries, 'Trolls are paupers and ne'er-do-wells!'

You search the trolls for booty and find the following. You may take one at most of the following items. Remember to write it on your adventure sheet.

A bag of **1D6** groats

A flint suitable for starting a fire

A skull. Probably from a human

Go to 400

341

You search a bleeding and still twitching goblin corpse and flinch with disgust as your fingers edge their way into their pockets and fish about. You find three items but you can choose only one to take with you.

Ashto groans, 'I can't believe we risked our lives for this!'

Make your choice and write it on your adventure sheet.

A child's wooden siege-engine toy

A mouldy handkerchief

Half a groat piece

Go to 404

342

Through the tree trunks, creepers and crisscrossing of webs you spy a nest of giant swamp spiders. They're huge, hairy and mottled, with their evil smell polluting the swamp.

Ashto moans, 'Spiders hate all of us dwarves! It doesn't matter how much we hunt them and drive them from our mines with firebrands

and pitchforks.'
Avoid? **Go to 17**
Greet? **Go to 364**
Attack? **Go to 409**

343

Ashto mumbles, 'The statues here are strange.'
Deduct **1** from your **Time** score. Out of time? **Go to 413**
Which way do you go next?
West? **Go to 275**
East? **Go to 282**
South? **Go to 266**

344

You try to strike the tree but it's protected by a powerful magic spell which reverses your own power back at you. Ashto points and laughs at you.

Roll **1D6** and subtract that from your **Strength** score. Dead? **Play again!** Alive?
Pluck? **Go to 74**
Leave? **Go to 397**

345

A beam of sunlight bursts out from the heavy clouds and warms your flesh as well as your soul in the gloom of the dark and fetid swamp. Roll **1D6** and add the result to your **Strength** score. Add **1** to your **Time** score.

Ashto scratches at his beard and chuckles, 'For once time is not our enemy! We must leave time behind us!' **Go to 208**

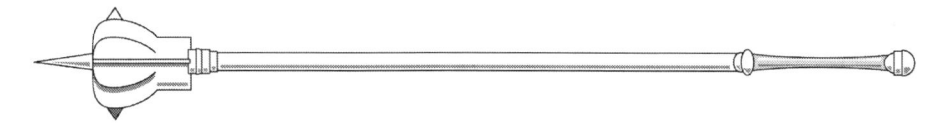

346

The sheriff throws his arms around with relief as you agree to fight the Bone Baron. He hands you a leather bag full of groats and then gives Ashto an equally full bag.

Roll **1D6** and multiply by **10**. Add this number of groats to your adventure sheet.

Ashto groans, 'Are you mad? We can't defeat the Bone Baron! That goblet belongs to me! I was instrumental in recovering it!'

There are screams and suddenly the throng of villagers stop pushing past you and turn to race for the safety of the village, chased by the charging Skeleton Horde! Leading the charge is the Bone Baron

Ashto screams, 'The goblet is only effective if you drink alcohol from it before combat! You must drink from the Goblet of Zakzak!'

What alcohol do you have to put into the goblet?

Ale? **Go to 85**
White wine? **Go to 360**
Red wine? **Go to 69**
If you have no alcohol, **go to 276**

347

The minstrel swings up their lute to use as a makeshift club! Ashto pretends to be a sparrow flitting about the ground. Fight!

The Minstrel

Initial attack score: **9**

Weapon damage: **4**

Strength: **4**

Lose? **Play again!** Win? **Go to 339**

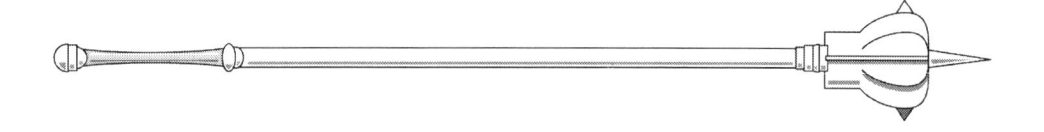

348

Ashto scurries away as fast as possible. **Go to 274**

349

The goblins are warriors and are always ready for a ruckus. Ashto farts loudly and excessively.

Fight each goblin scout in turn! They're armed with evil-looking daggers. If you have a vial of Griffdum you can throw it at one goblin and it will kill them instantly. Don't forget to remove the vial from your adventure sheet. As soon as you kill the first goblin you may add their dagger to your adventure sheet and use it in combat.

Goblin 1

Initial attack score: **7**

Weapon damage: **3**

Strength: **6**

Goblin 2

Initial attack score: **8**

Weapon damage: **3**

Strength: **7**

Goblin 3

Initial attack score: **9**

Weapon damage: **3**

Strength: **8**

Lose? **Play again!** Win? **Go to 280**

350

The goblins don't see you and you carry on your journey. Ashto is fanning themselves to cool down. **Go to 404**

351

You never imagined spiders were so evil and so smelly. Ashto curses, spits on the ground and declares, 'In dwarf legends, giant spiders were created by Xullu, the god of dwarves, the Most Major Miner, who discovered a party of dwarves who'd snuck into Xullu's Eternal Caverns in search of holy gold.

'And Xullu punished them by changing them into giant spiders. The real punishment is not being able to dig for gold ever again. No opposable thumbs you see. Otherwise, I can almost see the advantages of having eight legs. You'd never have to worry about orcs and goblins ever again for one thing!'

Deduct **1** from your **Time** score. Out of time? **Go to 413**
Which way do you go next?
West? **Go to 233**
East? **Go to 147**
South? **Go to 375**

352

Ashto mumbles, 'Time is not waiting for us! We must make all haste!'

Deduct **1** from your **Time** score. Out of time? **Go to 413**
Which way do you go next?
South? **Go to 122**
North? **Go to 126**
West? **Go to 133**

353

You attack the chest but it's protected by a powerful magic spell which blasts you to the ground. Ashto regards you with unremitting disdain.

Deduct **1D6** from your **Strength** score. Dead? **Play again!**
Alive? What do you do next?

Investigate? **Go to 114**
Leave? **Go to 170**

354

The witch has seen you! She extends a claw-like hand and beckons you to her.
Chat? **Go to 60**
Attack? **Go to 334**

355

The brigand points south into the swamp and cries|, 'That way lies the Goblet of Zakzak. But doom and disaster is all it brings! It's foretold! Beware the Goblet of Zakzak and beware the emerald fairy!'
Leave? **Go to 330**
Attack? **Go to 262**

356

Test your **Dexterity**. Roll **2D6**. How does this score compare to your **Dexterity**?
Equal or higher? **Go to 162**
Lower? **Go to 173**

357

The silver key fits perfectly and turns smoothly in the lock. At the bottom of the iron box a small hidden door flips open and spits groats at your feet. Before you can react the door snaps shut again.

Roll **5D6** to determine how many groats you've received. **Go to 120**

358

The clouds begin to race past at an unnatural speed and you're overcome by waves of nausea which cause you to collapse to the ground. Ashto vomits on the ground.
Roll **1D6** and deduct the result from your **Strength**. Dead? **Play again!**
Roll **1D6** and deduct the result from your **Time** score. Out of time? **Go to 413**
Alive? **Go to 23**

359

Ashto looks on disapprovingly. You grasp the fruit but the fruit gods are in a mischievous fettle! Grasping the fruit feels like putting your hand in a furnace! Deduct **2** from your **Strength** score. Dead? **Play again!** Alive? What do you do?
Pluck? **Go to 74**
Leave? **Go to 397**
Attack? **Go to 344**

360

You pour a measure of white wine into the goblet and then putting the goblet to your lips, guzzle the ale down. Immediately you feel a surge of magical power flow through your body.

During combat, instead of rolling **2D6** to calculate your **Attack Score**, roll **3D6**.

The sheriff hands you a longsword and taking the formidable weapon, you march forwards to confront the Bone Baron!

From behind you, Ashto shouts, 'Best of luck, look out for me in the afterlife!' And the dwarf runs away. **Go to 230**

361

The wooden faun creaks as it raises its sword even higher as it prepares to strike you! **Go to 73**

362

You try to strike the sundial but it's protected by a powerful magic spell which reverses your own power back at you. Ashto looks at you despairingly.

Roll **1D6** and deduct it from your **Strength**. Dead? **Play again!**

Alive? You need at least **1** groat to play this game. Remember to deduct it from your adventure sheet.

Play? **Go to 328**

Leave? **Go to 253**

363

The plinth is protected by a powerful magic spell and as you strike it you're assaulted by an invisible force which smacks you to the ground and leaves you stunned. Ashto wags a finger at you.

Roll **1D6** and deduct it from your **Strength**.

Dead? **Play again!** Alive? Continue.

(Remember you need at least **1** groat to pay tribute. Remember to deduct **1** groat from your adventure sheet. If you have no groats you must leave.)

Leave? **Go to 104**

Tribute? **Go to 207**

364

The giant swamp spiders chirp as they scramble towards you on their thick hairy legs, their stink is almost overpowering in its intensity. The most bloated spider trills, 'You smell good enough to fight over!'

Chat? **Go to 321**

Attack? **Go to 409**

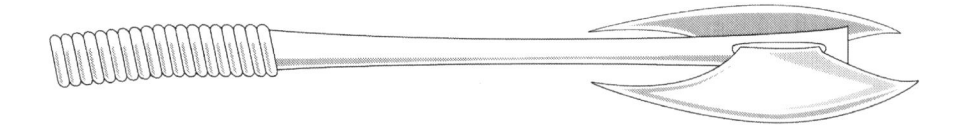

365

Test your **Dexterity**. Roll **2D6**. How does this score compare to your **Dexterity**?

Equal or higher? **Go to 337**

Lower? **Go to 350**

366

The minstrel smiles cheerfully and slaps you on the back before crying happily, 'Let the gods rejoice! I'm thrilled to meet you! For a small charitable donation, I shall share with you the gossip of the swamp to set you on your merry way!'

Ashto pulls out a pair of spoons from his pocket and begins tunelessly tapping out a rhythm.

If you wish to hear news of the swamp it will cost you one groat. Remember to deduct this from your adventure sheet.

News? **Go to 264**
Leave? **Go to 399**
Attack? **Go to 347**

367

The orcs quickly surround you and level their bloodied swords at you.

Confess? **Go to 325**
Attack? **Go to 237**

368

The most blotched and malodorous spider waves a diseased leg at you and trills, 'There are many humans in the swamp these days, they're all running from some big misfortune that is about to befall their lands. But it makes easy pickings for us! We like travellers through our swamp! Especially the females, eggs on legs we call them!'

Attack? **Go to 409**
Leave? **Go to 17**

369

Ashto pulls at his beard and cries, 'Nothing good was ever found rooting about on an orc's cadaver!'

You search the orcs for plunder and may take one of the following items. Remember to write it on your adventure sheet.

A brass ring
A WAR HAMMER
A gold key
Go to 319

370

The minstrel smiles warmly and shakes your hand vigorously before crying, 'Well met, merry strangers! For a small consideration, I shall gladden your hearts with a merry tune to set you on your merry way!'

Ashto sticks his hands deep in his pockets. If you wish to hear a tune it will cost you **1** groat. Remember to deduct this from your adventure sheet.

Tune or Tale? **Go to 212**
Leave? **Go to 67**
Attack? **Go to 148**

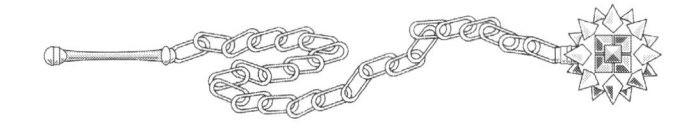

371

The goblins change direction to scuttle towards you. Small, wiry, snaggletoothed and filthy, they're covered in rough tattoos indicating their allegiance to the Bone Baron.

The dirtiest one looks you over and smirks, 'Are you old enough to be out by yourselves?'

As Ashto keeps a stony silence the other goblins heckle and jeer.
Chat? **Go to 386**
Leave? **Go to 404**
Attack? **Go to 317**

372

Among the teeming mass of terrified people you manage to find the sheriff, who's struggling to find anyone to help him defend Pigginmud from imminent assault by the Bone Baron and the Skeleton Horde. A look of desperate hope crosses this face when he sees you. He gasps, 'Do you have it?'

As you pull the goblet from your backpack the sheriff falls to his knees and praises the nine gods for this mercy. Then he stands up and implores, 'You are the finder of the goblet, you are our hero, you have the greatest chance of defeating the Bone Baron! You are our champion! The chosen one! Please, you must choose to help us defeat the Bone Baron, and save us all!'

Ashto pulls his beard and snarls, 'We just want the groats. We're not heroes. Where are our groats?'
Help? **Go to 346**
Leave? **Go to 292**

373

Ashto rolls his eyes. You grasp the fruit but the fruit gods are in a mischievous fettle! Grasping the fruit feels like picking up an old sock! Suddenly the fruit collapses into a soggy pulpy mess and maggots start crawling out of it!

Deduct **1** from your **Charisma** score.

Pluck? **Go to 74**

Leave? **Go to 397**

Attack? **Go to 344**

374

The forester rests on his enormous double-headed axe and beckons you forward. 'What are you two scoundrels doing in my garden?'

Ashto quivers behind you.

Chat? **Go to 327**

Leave? **Go to 54**

Attack? **Go to 162**

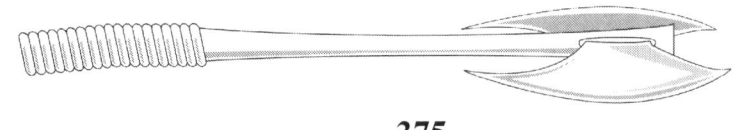

375

In a gap between the trees stands a nine-sided stone plinth. Ashto mutters, 'It's criminal to leave a nice bit of masonry like that about. Very careless.'

Avoid? **Go to 403**

Investigate? **Go to 301**

Attack? **Go to 277**

PORTAL

376

You're ambushed by a party of goblin scouts and as you attempt to defend yourself Ashto runs off into the trees and disappears.

Fight each goblin scout in turn. They're armed with evil-looking daggers. If you have a vial of Griffdum you can throw it at one goblin and it will kill them instantly. Don't forget to remove the vial from your adventure sheet.

As soon as you kill one goblin you may pick up their dagger and use it in combat. Remember to add it to your adventure sheet.

Goblin 1
Initial attack score: **7**
Weapon damage: 3
Strength: **6**
Goblin 2
Initial attack score: **8**
Weapon damage: **3**
Strength: **7**
Goblin 3
Initial attack score: **9**
Weapon damage: **3**
Strength: **8**
Dead? **Play again!** Win? **Go to 9**

377

Among the goods the villages have abandoned as they flee their homes is an ancient and empty cart being pulled along by a remarkably skinny pair of oxen.

Jumping aboard you grab the reins and steer it away from the approaching Skeleton Horde. In the disorderly rout, several elderly villagers fall beneath the hooves of your oxen and their screams are terrible to behold as they perish beneath the hoods of our beasts.

Ashto screams, 'Get out of the way, you idiots!'

You steer away path into the trees beyond the village and looking over your shoulder you see a red mist rise above Pigginmud as the Skeleton Horde descend upon the defenceless villagers.

Ashto counts his groats and scowls, 'I can't believe this is all we were paid! It's criminal what thieves are paid these days.'

Which way do you steer?

Left? **Go to 183**
Right? **Go to 376**
Straight ahead? **Go to 64**

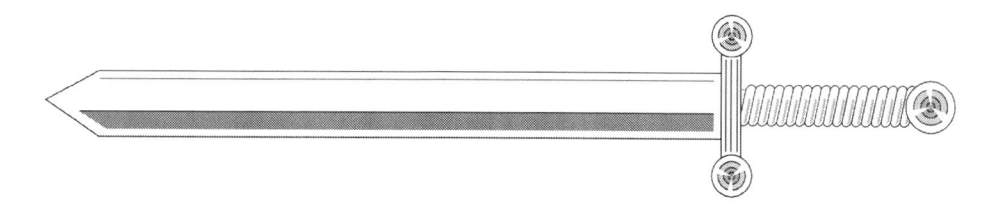

378

The orcs are highly trained fighting machines. And cruel with it. They don't know the meaning of the word 'mercy'. Or 'onomatopoeia'.

Ashto pretends to be hit by an arrow and staggers across the battleground before falling over, groaning excessively and pretending to be dead.

As soon as you kill the first orc you may pick up their shortsword and use it in combat. Don't forget to add it to your adventure sheet.

Orc warrior 1

Initial attack score: **14**

Weapon damage: **9**

Strength: **9**

Orc warrior 2

Initial attack score: **15**

Weapon damage: **9**

Strength: **10**

Orc Warrior 3

Weapon damage: **9**

Initial attack score: **16**

Strength: **11**

Dead? **Play again!** Win? **Go to 52**

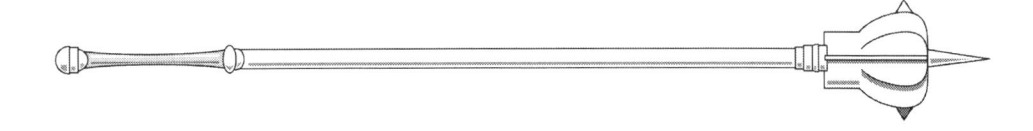

379

The branches of the ancient tree are laden with succulent apples, oranges and bananas. Ashto says, 'I am partial to a banana.'

Pluck? **Go to 145**

Leave? **Go to 324**

Attack? **Go to 80**

380

The minstrel has spotted you! Ashto punches your arm and says, 'Your fault!'.
Greet? **Go to 366**
Attack? **Go to 347**

381

The branches of the ancient tree are weighed down with ripe apples, oranges and bananas. Ashto says, 'Oh, get me a banana.'
Pluck? **Go to 74**
Leave? **Go to 397**
Attack? **Go to 344**

382

The rain finally stops and the mist clears to reveal a gang of orcs resting by a silver elm tree. They're heavily armed and decorated in the livery of the Bone Baron. Ashto mutters, 'Death to orcs! Death! Death I say!'
Avoid? **Go to 65**
Greet? **Go to 283**
Attack? **Go to 237**

383

The wizard laughs and says, 'Never attack a wizard!' And he throws up his right hand as if about to conjure a spell. And as you're hypnotised by his movement his staff sweeps around in a fluid arc and smites you accurately on the skull, verily but hard.

Deduct **2** from your **Strength** score. Dead? **Play again!**

Alive? Then the wizard disappears in a puff of green smoke. And Ashto regards you with maximum scorn. **Go to 229**

384

Test your **Dexterity**. Roll **2D6**. How does this score compare to your **Dexterity**?

Equal or higher? **Go to 215**

Lower? **Go to 348**

385

The brigand has spotted you! Roll **2D6**. How does this score compare to your **Charisma**?

Lower? **Go to 194**

Equal or higher? **Go to 262**

386

The dirtiest goblin leers, 'No one can stop the Bone Baron, the rider of the Freak dragon, not now they have the support of the Genio Divinitus!'

Leave? **Go to 349**

Attack? **Go to 317**

387

The spiders scuttle forward to attack you. Ashto furiously digs himself a small trench in the ground, climbs into it and covers all but his nostrils and eyes with the loose soil as you fight.

Fight each swamp spider in turn. If you possess a jar of Sogweed you may smash it on the ground. The fumes are poisonous to spiders and will cause the over-sized arachnids to scatter. **Go to 59** and remember to deduct the Sogweed from your adventure sheet.

If you have no Sogweed or you choose not to use it, you must fight.

Giant swamp spider 1
Initial attack score: **6**
Weapon damage: **5**
Strength: **21**

Giant swamp spider 2
Initial attack score: **7**
Weapon damage: **5**
Strength: **20**

Giant swamp spider 3
Initial attack score: **5**
Weapon damage: **5**
Strength: **19**

Dead? **Play again!** Win? **Go to 169**

388

The witch spins her broomstick around in her hands and adopts a fighting stance as the bristle-end of the broomstick snaps to a horizontal halt underneath one armpit and with the sharpened end pointing at you! Ashto closes his eyes. Fight!

Witch

Initial attack score: **14**

Weapon damage: **5**

Strength: **11**

Dead? **Play again!** Win? **Go to 274**

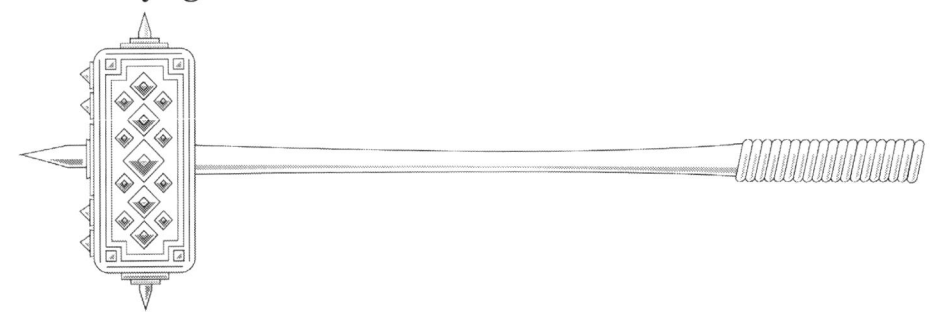

389

Test your dexterity. Roll **2D6**. How does this score compare to your **Dexterity**?

Equal or higher? **Go to 385**

Lower? **Go to 220**

390

The trolls have seen you and are pointing at you licking their lips before lumbering across to your position.

Chat? **Go to 123**

Attack? **Go to 94**

391

Ashto pulls at his beard and screams, 'Time is our mortal enemy! We must murder time!'
Deduct **1** from your **Time** score. Out of time? **Go to 413**
Which way do you go next?
South? **Go to 322**
North? **Go to 332**
West? **Go to 342**

392

You hand a groat to the emerald fairy who smiles, bows and says, 'Are you a devout follower of the eternal faun? You're about to be tested. The faithless will be punished and the devoted rewarded.'

Test your **Charisma**. Roll **2D6**. How does this score compare to your **Charisma**?
Lower? **Go to 70**
Equal or higher? **Go to 361**

393

You hear many large beasts splashing through the swamp, bellowing, hooting and roaring, and trampling the vegetation. You and Ashto exchange glances, wordlessly leave the path and plunge into the reeds and bullrushes to your left.

You wade as fast as you can through the waist-high stinking water until you think you've reached a safe distance from whatever the creatures were.

You reach a clearing between some willow trees and drag yourself up onto dry land.

An ancient lichen-covered stone sundial stands balanced on a crumbling stone pedestal at the centre of the clearing.

Ashto mutters, 'This is a place of powerful magic.'

Avoid? **Go to 284**
Investigate? **Go to 303**
Attack? **Go to 362**

394

There's a sharp click! A tiny dart flies out of the lock mechanism and stings you. Ashto regards you with sneering disgust.

Deduct **1D6** from your **Strength** score. Dead? **Play again!**
Alive? **Go to 170**

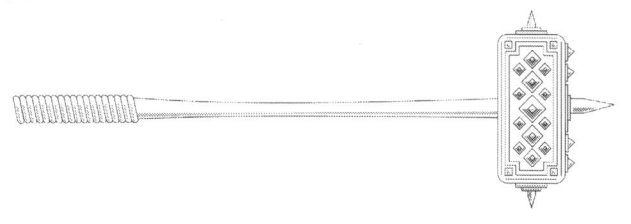

395

A sudden hailstorm sees you seek cover under the boughs of a tall larch tree. Ashto mutters, 'Stupid, stupid weather.'

Deduct **1** from your **Time** score. Out of time? **Go to 413**

Which way do you go next?

North? **Go to 53**
West? **Go to 68**
East? **Go to 63**

396

Test your **Dexterity**. Roll **2D6**. How does this score compare to your **Dexterity**?

Equal or higher? **Go to 201**

Lower? **Go to 141**

397

Ashto pulls at his beard and grumbles, 'Time is ticking! We must move onwards!'

Deduct **1** from your **Time** score. Out of time? **Go to 413**

Which way do you go next?

South? **Go to 233**

North? **Go to 147**

East? **Go to 375**

398

The poison gas is steadily rising and Ashto is coughing prodigiously and to your mind, somewhat theatrically. Deduct **1** from your **Strength** score. Dead? **Play again!**

Alive? Taking a deep breath you lean down and wedge your fingers into the slight crack where the stone door meets the tiled floor, and then straining every muscle you heave at the door to try and raise it open!

As Ashto coughs and wheezes, he regards you with undisguised disgust. Test your **Strength**. Roll **4D6**. How does this score compare to your **Strength score**?

Equal or higher? **Go to 136**

Lower? **Go to 238**

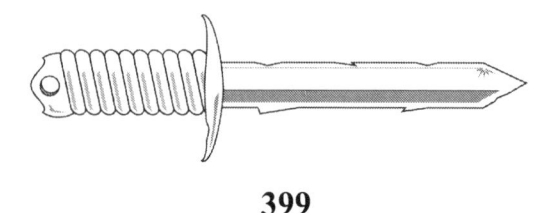

399

Ashto scratches at his beard and groans, 'Time is a leaky cauldron! We must repair urgently to our destination!'

Deduct **1** from your **Time** score. Out of time? **Go to 413**

Which way do you go next?

South? **Go to 375**

East? **Go to 233**

West? **Go to 147**

400

A sudden rainstorm sees you seek cover under the leaves of a large gorse bush. Ashto mutters, 'Gorse! I ask you.'

Deduct **1** from your **Time** score. Out of time? **Go to 413**

Which way do you go next?

East? **Go to 322**

South? **Go to 93**

West? **Go to 342**

401

Do you have a diamond ring to use as protection?
Yes? **Go to 125**
No? **Go to 178**

402

You drop a groat into the stone slot and a bright green flame bursts from the nozzle on top of the plinth and you make swipe at it.

Test your **Dexterity**. Roll **2D6**. How does this score compare to your **Dexterity**?
Lower? **Go to 13**
Equal or higher? **Go to 27**

403

Test your **Dexterity**. Roll **2D6**. How does this score compare to your **Dexterity**?
Equal or higher? **Go to 139**
Lower? **Go to 259**

404

Ashto yells, 'Make haste, the gods are not making time, they're spending it!'
Deduct 1 from your Time score. Out of time? **Go to 413**
Which way do you go next?
North? **Go to 208**
East? **Go to 63**
South? **Go to 48**

405

You carry on your journey, wondering how many more orcs are wandering the land. Ashto curses and says, 'We must murder every orc we encounter!'

Deduct **1** from your **Time** score. Out of time? **Go to 413**

Which way do you go next?

North? **Go to 26**

East? **Go to 256**

West? **Go to 247**

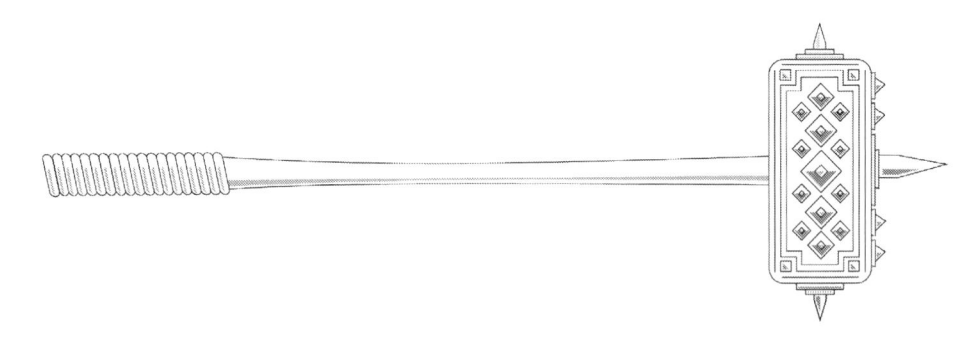

406

You search the forester and find three items. You can choose only one to take with you. You may take nothing if you wish. Ashto groans, 'It was so foolish to risk our lives for this. This!'

Make your choice:

A small vial of Griffdum

An **AXE**

A small jar of Howlmeat

Go to 54

407

Ashto yells, 'Time hates us!'

Deduct **1** from your **Time** score. Out of time? **Go to 413**

Which way do you go next?

East? **Go to 266**

West? **Go to 275**

North? **Go to 282**

408

Ashto scratches at his beard and mutters, 'Time is beyond us! We must get hasty!'

Deduct **1** from your **Time** score. Out of time? **Go to 413**

Which way do you go next?

North? **Go to 21**

South? **Go to 23**

West? **Go to 29**

409

The spiders scuttle forward to attack you. Ashto curls into a ball, grabs his ankles and rolls away bum over heels.

Fight! If you possess a jar of Sogweed you may smash it on the ground. The fumes are poisonous to spiders and will cause the over-sized arachnids to scatter. **Go to 351** and remember to deduct the Sogweed from your adventure sheet.

If you have no Sogweed, you must fight.

Giant swamp spider 1

Initial attack score: **7**

Weapon damage: **5**

Strength: **22**

Giant swamp spider 2

Initial attack score: **8**

Weapon damage: **5**

Strength: **20**

Giant swamp spider 3

Initial attack score: **8**

Weapon damage: **5**

Strength: **19**

Dead? **Play again!** Win? **Go to 331**

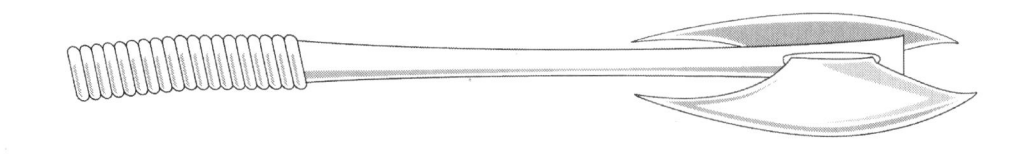

410

The Bone Baron lies dead at your feet, and with her death, the Skeleton Horde, which depended upon her vitality for their existence crumble to dust and are blown away in the breeze.

Write on your adventure sheet you've killed the Bone Baron.

The surviving villagers of Pigginmud run forth to hoist you on their shoulders and carry you to the village where they parade you about before bathing your wounds and hastily fashioning a feast with great quantities of ale, wine and pig meat accompanied by song, dance and tales of your heroism!

You've done it! You've endured the Swamp of Nok and lived to tell the tale, earned yourself a handsome reward in groats, saved the lives of the people of Pigginmud and earned their eternal gratitude and respect! Add **1D6** to your **Charisma** score and add **10D6** groats to your adventure sheet. **Go to 414**

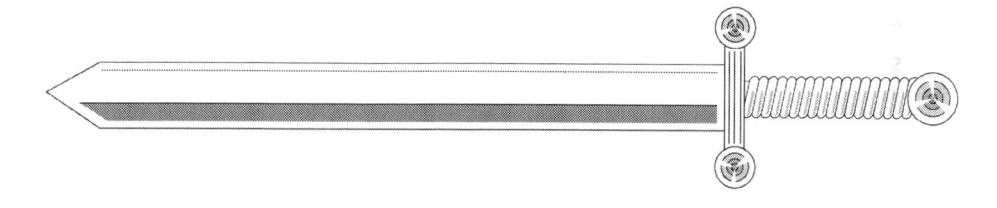

411

You hurry far away from Pigginmud and the Swamp of Nok. Note on your adventure sheet, you did not defeat the Bone Baron.

Eventually, you reach a crossroads far from the screams of Pigginmud. Ashto slaps your shoulder and says, 'Right then, I'm off. Happy trails, Andi, stay safe. And good luck.'

Ashto bows low and cries, 'I'll see you in Tickscab!' And with a grin, he scurries away as fast as he can. **Go to 414**

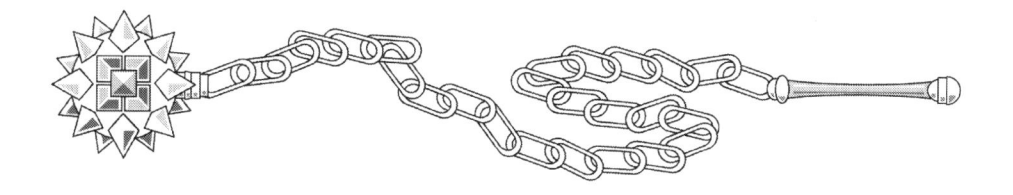

412

You edge further along the plank. Test your **Dexterity**. Roll **2D6**. How does this score compare to your **Dexterity**?
Equal or higher? **Go to 240**
Lower? **Go to 79**

413

Ashto shrugs and says, 'Oh well, I guess that's the end of Pigginmud. There's no point continuing this quest if there's no one left alive to pay us, eh? Right then, I'm off. Happy trails, Andi, stay safe. And good luck.'

Mark on your adventure sheet that you didn't return the Goblet of Zakzak to Pigginmud, and you didn't defeat the Bone Baron.

Ashto bows low and cries, 'I'll see you in Tickscab!' And with a grin, he scurries away as fast as he can. A cold wind blows against you.
Go to 414

GIANT SWAMP SPIDER

Congratulations!

You've survived the Swamp of Nok. Spend your groats quickly, for war is coming..

THE END

Also available
Game of Runes Book 2: Marsh of Mayhem
Game of Runes Book 3: Forest Infernal
Game of Runes Book 4: Death of Noking
Nemo's Fury
Nemo's Fury 2: Octo War

Game of Runes is also available as an online game for desktops, laptops and tablets: @ tinyurl.com/GameOfRunes

Join the mysterious Captain Nemo on board his remarkable submarine the Nautilus and experience a wild underwater voyage of monsters, mayhem and murder!

Thank you for playing Game of Runes, please look out for more games coming soon at **Gameofrunes.com**

Printed in Great Britain
by Amazon